THE

MAGIC

COIN

JOHN GOWANS

The Magic Coin
Copyright © 2020 by John Gowans

Tellwell Talent
www.tellwell.ca

ISBN
978-0-2288-4191-3 (Paperback)

This book is dedicated to my family,
who encouraged me while I pursued this dream,
and to my wife, Carol, whose love and support
inspired me to complete it.

CHAPTER 1

*I*T WAS SEPTEMBER 6. Already the carefree days of summer, which so recently had seemed like they would go on forever, were retreating as if into an impenetrable fog, soon to become only memories. Nancy De Bruin looked critically at herself in the hall mirror. She nodded her head in a slow up and down motion, and her dark curls moved across her shoulders in an affirmative manner. Her oval green eyes gave the reflected image approval: hair, makeup, clothes, shoes. Perfect. Ready for first day at Timespan High School, Nancy placed her favourite necklace around her neck—a gold coin with a curious triangle notch in it.

Stepping outside onto the porch of her family home, she closed her eyes and took a deep breath. *Okay*, she thought, *this is all going to work out fine this year*. Opening her eyes, she caught sight of her cousin, who was waiting at the end of the path.

1

"Oh, hey, Sam!" she called, giving a wave.

Even though they were cousins, Samuel De Bruin had also been Nan's best friend since kindergarten.

"Hey, Nan," he called back in his husky voice. As Nancy drew near, he smiled. "Wow, you look terrific!"

At sixteen, Sam was tall and slim. His blond hair, which hung around his face, looked a bit wild, but his clear blue eyes always hinted at adventure and a little bit of mischief. Sam had always been drawn to the ocean and had competed in the Malibu teen surf rider competition.

Nan smiled back at her cousin. "Thanks, Sam. Are you as nervous as I am?" The two began walking toward their new school.

"Not at all, Nan," said Sam. "This new school is a brand-new start for us, and good riddance to Calvin Fishbone Jr. High."

They walked along in silence for a few minutes.

"Do you think our teachers will be nice, Sam?"

Sam shared his cousin's anxiety about the new school but didn't want to let her know that. "Don't worry, Nan. I'm sure they'll be awesome."

As they turned the corner, Timespan High School came into sight. Built in 1896, the building was a mixture of architectural styles that gave the school a magical, castle-like appearance. The large thirty-foot turret on the west side had a red flag with a yellow dragon emblazoned on it. On the east side, a square tower rose three storeys high, its roofline of castle-like granite blocks giving it a military look. Across the middle, spanning seventy feet and joining the two, was a two-storey red brick building with a fifteen-foot gothic arched door in the centre. The grounds were surrounded by a ten-foot tall stone wall, and over the large wrought iron gate were the words "Enter All Who Seek Knowledge." It was an intimidating sight, one in which the very building itself seemed to question whether the cousins had the courage to accept the unknown adventure that lay before them.

Sam and Nan stopped dead in their tracks and just stared. His heart pounding, Sam felt just like he did when a powerful wave approached him, and he knew if he mishandled it, he would be tossed into the air like a ragdoll. Nancy, feeling her stomach tightening and her body going cold, knew if she tried to speak, she would have no voice. All around them students were streaming into the school, chatting, laughing, and delighted to see their friends after the summer. They were seemingly oblivious to two new kids and the building. Sam felt Nancy's hand grip his arm. He straightened up and tried to look confident.

"Come on, Nancy, it's gonna be okay."

Sam entered the school through the huge double doors beneath the gothic arch. Looking up, he shuddered at the leering gargoyle affixed overhead. Nan had gone in ahead of Sam and was transfixed in the centre of the foyer as she struggled to take in the enormity of the space. Overhead, an ancient chandelier hung from a large wooden beam. The fixture was eight feet in diameter and twelve feet in height and was made up of interlocking trident spears and other mythical images. The walls, which seemed to Nan to go on forever, were finished in dark oak panelling, and a large staircase rose to the second floor.

The whole room would have seemed quite creepy had it not been for the happy noise of all the other students. The energy and excitement level were so infectious that the two friends weren't as overwhelmed as they could have been, but it *was* the first day of school and they were anxious.

"You two look lost." The voice belonged to a tall, rather gangly guy with a mop of unruly black curls and a thin, rather unpleasant, angular face. "I'm Jake. Can I help you find your class?"

Nancy answered quickly. "Yes, and thanks. I'm Nancy De Bruin, and this is my cousin Sam."

Sam stepped forward. "Hey, good to meet ya."

Jake responded to Sam's fist bump, but his eyes darkened as he connected. "Jake Van Eck. My real name is Jacob, but everyone calls me Jake. So what grade are you both in?"

"We're both in ten," Sam answered.

"Ten works for me," Jake replied. "That's my grade; let's go upstairs to homeroom. Bell's about to ring."

Jake took the stairs two at a time with the ease of an antelope. His long legs gave him an advantage over Nancy, who had to hustle to keep up. Sam, not to be outdone, tried to do the stairs three at a time to pass Jake, but he tripped and sprawled onto the top landing just as he was about to pass him.

"You okay?" Jake asked, looking down at Sam without offering to help him up.

"No worries, I'm fine." Sam looked angry as he glanced at Nancy.

"Quite an entrance, tough guy." Nancy smiled at her cousin. Sam said nothing as he stood up and tried to regain his sense of composure. Glaring at Jake, he was convinced he'd been deliberately tripped.

The three students walked down the long corridor in silence, Sam limping slightly.

"I think you just met the ghost of Timespan High," Jake said lightly. "It's been said that there's a spirit that roams the hallways and doesn't care for newcomers."

Before either Sam or Nancy could reply, they arrived at their classroom and went in. As Jake passed Nancy, he took a long sideways look at her pendant, and his face seemed to harden. Sam glanced down the long hallway and saw an imposing door, which he presumed opened into the turret. Looking a little harder, it was the light he saw coming from under the door that troubled him, but he had no time to check it out, as class was beginning and he had to go in.

CHAPTER 2

THE CLASSROOM CONSISTED OF twenty single student desks arranged in a semi-circle two deep.

The professor's desk, which was quite large and piled high with stacks of books, was placed in the front of the class in the corner facing the semi-circle. A large old-fashioned blackboard was affixed to the front wall, and the school flag with the dragon in the centre was standing beside it in the corner. A bank of windows running along the wall let in natural light.

Sam and Nancy slid into the first available desks they could find in the back row and tried not to react to the stares of the students already seated. Jake, nodding acknowledgement to some friends, sat right in front of them. Nancy was relieved that she could sit with Sam, and as she looked around the classroom, she noticed a man partially hidden behind the piles of books. He was looking thoughtfully at the two new students. The professor stood up to address the class. He was short and rather plump, and a pair of round black glasses framed his dark eyes, giving his face an owlish appearance.

"The Golden Age of Holland," he began. "Please open your textbooks to page five."

Sam opened his textbook but couldn't take his mind off the eerie green light coming from behind the turret door, and what Jake had said about a spirit roaming the school. *Probably just a practical joke*, he thought. Or was it?

Nancy was absorbing her surroundings, absentmindedly playing with the coin on her chain. The professor looked strangely familiar. Where had she seen him before? Could it have been a resemblance to the old painting in the entry? Nancy was puzzling this as the lesson went on. He was speaking of the Golden Age as one who seemed to have been there himself, and he was interesting enough, but Nancy was thinking about something else and had a hard time concentrating. All at once she became aware of the professor watching her. He held Nancy's gaze for a second before his eyes rested on the coin hanging around her neck. Looking back up at Nancy, his expression changed and his eyes reflected an intensity that unnerved the teen.

Nancy felt that she was connected to the professor in a significant way. *How could this be?* she thought. *I shouldn't know the professor, but he seems to be looking right through me and into my soul.* All at once, Nancy began to suspect that the professor wasn't who he appeared to be. She had experienced this feeling in the presence of her grandfather, Samuel De Bruin II. Opa, as he was known to the family, had always been a gentle man, and Nancy loved him dearly. Opa had a gift—he just seemed to know things. Nancy loved to go to his house and spend time over a cup of tea with him as she listened to stories of adventures from long ago. His house was filled with antiques, paintings, and furniture that were hundreds of years old. Nancy had asked Opa how he'd collected so many priceless things, and he had told her that they had been passed down through his family, which had originated in Holland. Sometimes he seemed to gaze at Nancy with a look that suggested he knew that his granddaughter had a destiny much greater than that of just an ordinary teen, a destiny to change history itself. One day when Nancy went for tea, Opa sat with her in the rocking chairs on the front porch.

"I have something for you, something powerful and very valuable," Opa began as he passed a necklace to Nancy.

"This is beautiful, Opa," Nancy said as she held the necklace up to the light. "The coin is so unusual."

"This is for you to always wear. It has been passed down through the De Bruin family for hundreds of years and is now yours. It's a rare gift, but it's yours because you're the one with the gifting to unlock the coin's power. One day, its true power will be revealed, but until then, keep it close and safe."

Nancy brushed her curls away from her eyes as she studied the coin. Without trying, she began to experience a strange attachment to the jewel. Nancy went to say something when Opa started singing softly over her and she fell into a deep sleep. When she awoke, Opa was looking at her with the same intense look as the professor, and she knew she had a special gift and that the coin was magic.

"The song can be used to unlock some of the magic of the coin," Opa explained. "Whenever you sense danger, you can use it to lull your adversary to sleep, and the magic will erase their memory of you."

"How will I know the words to sing?" Nancy asked as she shook her curls and tried to clear her head.

"The holder of the coin only needs to start to sing and the magic will produce the words. You'll learn to trust the coin; it will always respond to the holder, and the holder can decide how much of the magic is used."

Nancy was remembering this conversation when the professor's gaze shifted to her cousin Sam, now lost in his daydream. "Mr. De Bruin!" Sam woke with a start. "Come back after school today. You too, Miss De Bruin." The bell rang and the students arose. With an uproar of voices, they prepared to move to the next class.

"Great, our first day and already we have to come in after school," Nancy said with a sigh.

"Well, I plan on coming back anyway," Sam said, "to find out more about our roaming spirit! Come on, let's head to our next class; we'll meet Jake at the cafeteria for lunch."

The cafeteria at one time was the banquet hall. At one end was a massive fireplace that was fifteen feet wide and rose to the ceiling eighteen feet high. The open timbered ceiling structure was finished with fir planks painted white, and the beams were solid oak that had aged to a rich ebony. The walls were painted plaster and had a warm cream hue. The floors were oak and bore the marks of many travellers. This was an interior room with no windows, but the large ornate lighting fixtures and skylights overhead bathed the room in light.

A roar of sound filled the room as students vied for recognition in conversation. The chatter was quite pleasant to everyone, as it was a happy sound. Looking around at the tables and chairs that filled the room, Sam found a place near the middle and motioned to Nancy to sit down. Jake joined them.

Opening his backpack, Sam pulled out a sandwich and a coke. Nancy had packed some cold chicken and water, and Jake produced a feast of cold cuts, pastry, and a thermos of coffee.

"So what brought you here to this school?" Jake tucked into his lunch as he waited for an answer.

Sam glanced at Nan, his eyes taking on an icy blue tone that asked, "Can we trust him?"

Nancy was sure she shouldn't reveal their secret, so she danced around the question.

"We heard it was a good place. Now tell us about the spirit that doesn't like newcomers. Are you just making fun of us?" As she said this, the chandelier overhead started to swing slightly. Nancy shivered involuntarily.

"There's something you should know. You have to talk to the professor about this, but you're never allowed to enter the turret," said Jake.

"Why not?" Nan asked.

"Timespan is in the building built by a reclusive Dutchman believed to have hidden his wealth somewhere in the building. When he died, he willed the building to the city on the condition they operated it as a school and agreed to never change it." Jake laughed. "Maybe his spirit roams the school to protect his wealth! Just a lot of nonsense if you ask me! I think the professor just doesn't want anyone messing with his stuff!"

Sam said nothing but couldn't help asking himself: *What was it that I saw at the end of the hall by the turret?* He knew he would have to find out.

"I've got to get into that turret," Sam said to Nancy when they were alone.

"Oh Sam, what's with you and that turret? You heard what Jake said."

"Nancy, you've got to trust me. I saw something glowing under the turret door."

Nancy glared at her cousin. "You sure your imagination isn't working to get us expelled again? Besides, you know the professor told us to come back to his class after school. Let's just ask him why we can't go into the turret."

Sam nodded agreement, but inside his mind he was determining a way into the school when night fell. With or without Nancy, he was going in.

The professor was reviewing a paper when Sam and Nancy entered the room. Looking up, he nodded a greeting and motioned to the cousins to sit in the two chairs he'd placed in front of his desk. Once again, Nancy thought she recognized him. What was it? Her thoughts were interrupted.

"Welcome to Timespan. I'm glad you're here." The professor eyed the cousins with an intensity that seemed to suggest he knew them already. "I had heard we were going to be adding some new students this year, and I wanted to meet you."

"So we're not in trouble?" Sam asked.

"No, not at all." The professor laughed. "Tell me a bit about your family."

"My family roots go back to the Netherlands. I don't know everything, but my grandfather has told me stories of trade merchants in the family who made fortunes. Apparently, there was great wealth accumulated but much was never seen after the war." As Nancy spoke, her green eyes flashed, and she held her hand to the coin.

"And that piece of jewellery around your neck … what's the significance?"

"It's a family heirloom my grandfather gave to me."

"And you, Master De Bruin, what's your story?"

"Nancy and I are cousins. I was born here in California, and when I was thirteen, I won first place in the Malibu thirteen-to-fifteen-year surfing competition." Sam said this with more than a hint of pride. He was a strong swimmer and a good-looking guy, and surfing gave him a sense of accomplishment.

"And what about that unusual jewel you wear?" The professor was looking at the gold trident hanging around Sam's neck by a thin leather cord. The spear had three tips, but the middle one was in the shape of a triangle.

"This was given to me by my grandfather, who told me my love of the sea was part of my family heritage."

The professor just nodded and seemed lost in thought for a moment.

"Can I ask you something, Professor?" Sam asked.

"Of course."

"Why can't we ever go into the turret?"

"Whatever do you mean?"

"It's just something that I heard." Sam's blue eyes brightened. "I also heard that there was a ghost roaming Timespan High."

The professor didn't answer immediately but appeared thoughtful. Changing the subject, he asked Nancy, "May I have a closer look at the coin on your necklace?"

Nancy held the coin in her hand. The gold coin with the missing piece glowed brightly.

"This has been in my family for generations. I don't know what it is, but I was told it was very special."

The professor's eyes narrowed a bit as he studied it.

"I was told such a coin was in the city, and now I see it's true. I believe you both know more than you're saying, and that's a good thing. You must be careful, for there are many who would seek to possess it."

Nancy felt a chill as the professor talked. "What do you mean?" she asked as the professor looked directly into her green eyes.

"You're not here by accident. There are secrets to the past that have been locked away for centuries—secrets of power, wealth, and murder. These can only be revealed by a descendant, one who has the coin and the gifting but no greed inside them."

"I don't understand." Nancy asked this while giving the professor a questioning gaze.

Reaching for a thin volume from the bookcase, he opened the book and began to read: "Two shall come down through the age, one who holds the coin, the other who holds the trident spear. They shall unlock the past but shall not profit from it." The professor looked at Sam and Nancy. "You have the true gift to go back in time to reveal the secrets and expose them to the light."

CHAPTER 3

$\mathcal{T}$HE ONLY SOUND IN the room was the ticking antique mantel clock on the professor's desk. The pace of passing time was measured by the rhythmic sound. Nancy was the first to break the silence, speaking in a hushed voice: "Travel back in time?"

"Seriously?" Sam questioned, shaking his blond hair. "How do we do that?"

Without answering, the professor motioned for silence and in a low voice replied, "Follow me; some things are best to speak of where others cannot hear." And with that, he led them out of the classroom and turned toward the turret.

The door to the turret was heavy and oak-shaped, like a gothic arch. At the ends of the black hinges, which extended one-third of the way across the top and bottom, were crescent shaped extensions that looked like the triton's spearhead on Sam's chain. The handle was an elaborate ivy motif, and the lock was inset into the wood beneath it. Carved into the centre of the door and measuring twelve inches in circumference was a coin that was identical to Nancy's necklace.

The professor reached into his jacket pocket and withdrew two objects. The first was an oak triangle, which he fit perfectly into the coin on the door. The second was a bronze key, which was eight inches long. He inserted the key and turned it first to the left until a soft click was heard, and then to the right until another click was heard, and then in a one-hundred-and-eighty-degree turn, upon which the heavy door swung open noiselessly and a soft green light from within flooded the doorway.

"My gosh, the door lock is a combination lock!" Sam said with excitement in his voice. "And the door is a vault!"

"And the green light was your ghost!" Nancy added.

"Follow me quickly." The professor moved through the light and into the turret. The cousins followed, and the door to the turret began to close behind them.

The turret was about fifteen feet in diameter. The stone steps that spiralled up were immediately before them, and a stunning gothic window overlooked the stairwell. The window was a stain glass depiction of a beautiful tulip with striking flames of orange, red, and white running up the petals. The glass had been hand blown in a rich texture of royal blue, which set the tulip beautifully. Circling the entire perimeter of the window, written in calligraphy, was a message from an ancient language.

"The tulip in the glass was named Anna Fierus," the professor said as the cousins stopped to admire the window.

"What does the writing say?" Nancy asked.

The professor adjusted his glasses. "The one who lets honesty and goodness rule in their heart becomes victorious." He continued: "This single flower was the start of the ruin of the Van Eck fortune and the rise of the De Bruin family. It's also said to be the reason Van Eck vowed never to rest until De Bruin had been brought to ruin."

"And this is the ghost that roams the school?" Sam asked.

The professor, moving rapidly up the stairs, didn't answer, and the cousins had to hurry to keep up. When they reached the landing at the top of the stairs, they entered a large study. The ceiling was timber and soared twenty feet into a point, which was the top of the turret. A large fireplace with brick facing took up one wall, and the professor immediately went to light a fire in it. All the turret walls were covered with large tapestries ten feet tall and ten feet wide; these were hand-woven works of art depicting scenes of life in seventeenth-century Holland. There were four in total circling the room.

"These are meant to be read as a story of the four seasons in seventeenth-century Holland," the professor explained. "Summer, fall, winter, and spring. Tapestries were an important part of decorations from the 1600s to the 1800s. Not surprisingly, Dutch merchants played an important role in the distribution of the tapestries all over Europe. Brussels and Antwerp were the primary centres where weavers crafted the product. Many of the designs were painted by well known artists, and the weavers faithfully reproduced the painted works of art in cloth. Large looms were used to weave the tapestry using wool, cotton, silk, and even silver and gold. The tapestries had an additional use outside of decoration; they also covered drafty hallways in castles and could be rolled up and easily transported when the wealthy patrons and merchants moved around from castle to castle."

The cousins examined the tapestries more closely. Summer showed people in the fields and in stages of relaxation while ships were sailing up the Amstel River. The beautiful warm sunshine glowed a golden yellow, and the River Amstel shimmered with a silver hue. The blue sky and green grass looked inviting, and the people on the riverbank and small boats brought in a bounty of fish. Fall depicted the harvest, with people using scythes, which flashed silver in the bright yellow sunlight, cut the golden-brown hay. Oxen-drawn carts loaded with the golden hay headed to market, and in the forest, rich with green foliage, hunters pursued their game. Winter showed people skating on the river beside snow-covered banks. The silver ribbon of ice and the sparkling snow was entrancing. Happy people could be seen gathering around fires that burned a beautiful yellow flame as they enjoyed the winter festival. Overhead, a large silver moon drenched light on a distant caravan loaded with barrels, which made its way up a winding path toward a golden castle. Spring showed the farmers planting new crops in freshly tilled fields. Merchants were seen trading goods, made over the winter, on Amsterdam's city streets. The buildings in the city were yellow, white, blue, and red, and the sky was the golden yellow it turns at dawn.

"They're beautiful in colour and texture," Nancy said as she admired the detailed stitching.

"Hmmm, I guess they're all right," Sam said, clearly not as interested in the artwork as he was in the ghost lore.

As the cousins looked around, they noticed the leather and oak furniture, which was heavy in appearance and had inlayed tiles that appeared to be brass but with a golden shine to them. The furniture was arranged in a semi-circle facing the blazing fire, which was now giving a warm orange glow to the room. The mantle was also inlayed with tiles, and the objects on it were a lion, a clock, and a unicorn. The lion was about two feet long and one foot high. His body was painted a rich tan and his claws were polished metal. The clock, the chimes of which were miniature men with hammers ringing the bell, chimed four o'clock, and the face, which was silver, had gold Roman numerals. The unicorn, painted white and blue with emerald coloured eyes and a silver horn, finished the arrangement on the mantel.

The stone floors were covered in heavy area rugs made of wool. All of this would have made a very large impression on its own, but standing on an easel to the left of the fireplace was a painting that appeared to be three feet wide and four feet high. The handsome young man gazed out from the canvas with an intelligent, thoughtful countenance. His dark curls framed his rather elongated face, and the hat he wore was wide-brimmed and tall. His high cheekbones complemented his elegant nose, and his complexion had an added touch of blush to offset the pure white skin. The high white ruffled collar, which rose to just beneath his strong, square jaw, was the fashion style of the merchant class in 1635 Holland. To the right of the fireplace another easel was placed and held a painting of a similar size. A beautiful young woman with blonde hair looked out. Her blue eyes seemed to question nothing but ask everything. Her fair complexion was the colour of clouds, and her petite nose, which was turned up at the end, emphasized her bow-shaped mouth and rounded jaw. She was dressed in a light blue dress with a lace shawl draped on her shoulders. Nancy leaned in to examine the art more closely.

"Rembrandt," she whispered, looking at the undiscovered masterpieces.

"Anna De Bruin." The professor's voice was soft as Nancy absorbed this.

"And who is the young man?" Nancy asked.

"He is Jonathan Van Eck, son of Patron Van Eck." The professor paused for a moment, filled a pipe with tobacco, and slowly lit it as Sam continued to study the image of the young man.

"He kind of looks like Jake." Sam was intrigued.

"Hey, you're right, Sam, he sort of does," Nancy agreed.

"That guy is creepy if you ask me. I still say he tripped me." Sam said this disgustedly.

"It's okay, Sam," Nancy said as she sat down in one of the large leather chairs facing the fire. It was all so overwhelming, she felt she had to find out more. "Give the professor time to explain."

The professor sat in a chair and turned toward the paintings. "Magnificent, are they not?" He turned to face the cousins: "These have been hidden from the world for centuries, but the time has come to uncover the true story of Anna and Jonathan and the De Bruin rise of fortune. It's also time to determine the rightful owner of the masterpieces."

Nancy was anxious to know why they were there. "Sir, can you explain all of this?"

"There's much you have to learn about your powers." The professor said this as he selected a volume of works from the bookcase. "The magic coin and the trident were found under mysterious circumstances by Hans De Bruin sometime in the seventeenth century. The origins of the jewels are recorded in this ancient manuscript." The professor paused to look at Sam and Nancy, who were leaning slightly forward in order not to miss a thing. "There was a time in the Middle Ages when the land now known as Holland was at war. Two kings battled each other for the right to rule, and powerful families obtained significant wealth by force. During this time, a gold coin fashioned by a gifted craftsman who had magical powers was created as a gift for the king of the north. There was magic in this beautiful coin, which enabled its owner to prosper in everything they put their hand to. The king of the north, a good man, understood the power of the coin and made an alliance with the wealthy families of his kingdom, having them seek peace with each other. For many years the alliance held, and peace was over the land. The crops were strong and there was never a drought. Merchants were able to sell the merchandise they obtained for a profit and never a loss. The king valued the jewel highly."

Sam and Nancy hung on every word.

"Is there more to the power of the coin?" Nancy asked.

"What about the trident?" Sam, sitting forward in his chair, had the posture of one who looked ready to catch a wave.

"Yes, there's much more to the story." The professor settled back in his chair and continued to read the story. "The king of the south was given the trident, which was forged for the seafaring kings and created by craftsmen able to infuse it with great power. It was made of emeralds, sapphires, rubies, and diamonds, and it took on the look and colour of the sea. Great skill in seafaring ways was bestowed upon the owner of the trident, and through this, great wealth was accumulated for the king and the people of the south.

The coin and the trident had power, but they only worked when the holders were at peace. If either king tried to use his power to overthrow the other, the jewels would curse the holder. The king of the north and the king of the south formed a truce that allowed the two kingdoms to remain at peace for 130 years until the king of the north died. His kingdom went to his daughter, Princess Leah, who was married to a greedy man named Grimm. Grimm was envious of the south's power and wanted it for himself. He knew that he must possess the trident, but he didn't know the secret of the jewel's power. He thought that with the coin he could defeat the southern king's armies and obtain the trident, but what he didn't realize was that the coin would recognize good from evil, and in the hands of an evil person, it would only serve to bring misfortune on the holder.

Grimm set about to kidnap Princess Hannah, the daughter of the king of the south. She was a beautiful girl whom her father loved deeply. One summer night, Grimm and his followers broke into the southern castle and carried the girl away to a hideout in the north. The king of the south loved Hannah and agreed to exchange the trident for her life.

At daybreak the following morning, a confident Grimm rode to meet the king of the south. The king was a seafaring man, so it was agreed to meet on his best ship.

"You are here," growled an angry king.

"As agreed," said Grimm. "Now show me the trident."

"I see you're wearing the coin and the king's robes," spat out the angry king.

"Here it is." Grimm proudly held the coin up for all to see. "Now give me the trident, and I'll release your daughter."

"Show me Hannah first."

Grimm motioned to his men, who brought the girl to the king.

"And are you unharmed, my dear Hannah?" The concern on the king's face was clear.

"Yes, my Lord, I am untouched," Hannah replied, her voice trembling as she spoke.

"Very well then, here is your trident," he snarled, "and may it bring you no good."

The king gave the trident to Grimm, who held it up to the light. He was so engrossed with its beauty that he didn't even see the trap that had been laid for him. From every part of the ship, armed soldiers loyal to the king emerged. The noblemen loyal to Grimm tried to flee but found themselves surrounded. There had never been a fiercer battle fought than on that day. The sounds of metal swords striking one another rang out for hours, and the sound of screaming men was heard across the entire land. As the battle raged, blood stained the ship's decks, and the sea turned red. As the sun set, Grimm and the king faced each other.

"Grimm, you evil man," the king cried, "I vowed you wouldn't see tomorrow's dawn."

"You are an old fool!" answered Grimm. "It is you who will not see the sunset today!"

The two men fought on, and just when it seemed neither had strength to endure, the king ran Grimm through with his sword and ended the battle. When Grimm's followers saw that their leader had been slain, they surrendered and begged for mercy.

"Let them return to their homes," the king commanded. "They'll cause us no more trouble."

Standing on the blood-stained deck, the king called out, "Friends, for 130 years we have enjoyed peace, but I see now that the power of the jewels is too strong for many to resist. There will come a time when the right house will find them, but it is not for today." And he took the jewels and threw them into the sea, where they sank to the bottom of the ocean.

Grimm's wife, Princess Leah, was driven to madness with her loss. She continued to search for the jewels, spending all she had, and died alone and destitute. The power of the jewels had become a curse, but after the princess died, an uneasy peace fell over the land. Eventually, the kingdoms were united in 1437 and renamed Holland. Much of Holland was covered with water, so it was very marshy. The Dutch ingeniously began to reclaim the land from beneath the water by digging a system of canals and, using the dirt, built barriers known as dykes. This amazing feat of engineering resulted in land that was now dry and usable. However, unknown to the builders of the canals, two jewels were once again on dry land. The power of the jewels began to rekindle.

The professor closed the thin volume. Sam and Nancy felt they had actually been there at the battle.

"What an astonishing story!" Nancy said.

"Yes, it is an amazing story, but it's still incomplete." The professor looked directly at Sam and Nancy as he said this. "The power of the jewels began to grow in the hands of Hans. What he didn't know was that there were two other pieces of jewellery that were kept hidden from the kings by the craftsmen who'd made the coin and the trident. These other pieces were a coin that allowed the holder special power to travel through time, and a triangle to keep the holder safe.

"Is this the coin?" The anxious tone in Nancy's voice was rising.

"Yes, that's the coin, and the triangle on Sam's trident will complete it. When the coin is complete, you can travel back in time to find the missing jewels and reveal the truth behind what happened to Jonathan Van Eck, and the rise of the De Bruin empire. It was recorded that it was Jonathan Van Eck himself who, out of his great love for Anna, brought an end to the fortunes of the Van Eck family and a rise to the fortunes of the De Bruin family, but this was never proved. You, Miss De Bruin, are the one to go back in time to find the truth and bring it to the light."

"Back in time? What do you mean? How?" Nancy had a million questions.

"That coin that hangs around your neck was passed down from generation to generation until it hung around the neck of the one person who could unlock the magic. The matching triangle on Sam's trident, when joined to the coin, will complete the circle and send you back in time."

"So this is the magic coin?" Nancy was stunned.

"That's not the coin of prosperity and peace that you have around your neck, but it is the coin that allows you to time travel. Many have tried to find it. Can you imagine how the greedy and evil ones could use it?"

"I can imagine that," said Sam. "I could go back to last week's football game and make a fortune betting, because I already know the score!"

"Or you could go back one day and buy stocks you know would be higher a day later!" Nancy chimed in.

"There are many ways the coin could be used for evil and not for good; that's why the keeper of the triangle and the keeper of the coin are in separate places and must never be allowed to fall into the wrong hands!"

"So why exactly am I to go back in time?" Nancy was perplexed.

"There are several things for you to discover," said the professor. "You must bring back the coin and the trident to be held safely from the evil ones who would abuse the power. Along the way, you're to learn the truth of Jonathan and Anna, and of what happened to Van Eck. Finally, the question of Anika De Bruin and where she hid her gold must be revealed, as your family's fortune depends on it!"

"Her gold?" both cousins asked at the same time.

"Yes. Even though Hans was a good man, his wife, Anika, was a scheming, greedy woman. As the family prospered, she took much of the wealth and hid it away. Hans was always too busy to notice, but when she died, she took the secret to her grave. It has always been rumoured that Van Eck spent his days conspiring to steal it, but no one has ever known the truth."

Suddenly, Nancy knew where she had seen the professor. He was the subject in a painting that hung in her grandfather's living room. "You're the one in the painting in Opa's living room!" she exclaimed.

A smile briefly crossed the professor's lips. "Not me; that painting is your great uncle. I'm his nephew and have known your opa since we were children. We're the two in this family who have possessed the knowledge of the coin that has been passed down through the generations. Your opa was keeping the jewels safe for the one who could use them. When you were born, he and I both knew we could entrust you with the secret." Turning more serious, the professor continued. "You must know of your special powers. You can see things before they happen but haven't until recently been able to understand your gift. With the coin, you can travel in time and make time stand still. This power could only be released when the triangle and the coin could be joined by the one person who wouldn't steal the gift and use it only for themselves or evil. You are the one set to release the gift. No secret is ever hidden from sight; it's only ever hidden until the appointed time to release it."

Nancy and Sam stood quite still. The professor then held Sam in his gaze.

"You are the one to travel with her, for it was written that two shall unlock the mystery." Sam took the trident from around his neck and held it to the light. The triangle glowed brightly, and the coin around Nancy's neck turned a bright silver gold.

Nancy looked at her cousin. "The trident and the coin seem to sense each other. The magic is beginning."

"How will we know when to return to the twenty-first century?" Sam asked.

"Look for the signs; it's within your power. You'll know what to do, but be careful, for there are others who are willing to kill for the coin." Turning to Nancy, he produced a small green purse made of velvet. "There are nuggets of gold in here. Use them sparingly when you're asked for payment, and beware—many would rob you for this. Now, you will need clothes to wear."

The professor went to the large wardrobe that was standing against the wall and opened the door. Inside was an assortment of clothes from various periods of time.

"Come and pick some clothes to wear." He beckoned to the cousins.

"Don't you think we could go back and set a new fashion trend?" Sam joked.

Ignoring her cousin, Nancy picked a dark blue, long-sleeved plain cotton dress. The button up high-top shoes were black leather. For an accent, Nancy chose a lace cap and shawl. Sam chose a black jacket with tan britches and leather shoes with a large brass buckle.

"Ugh, I feel like I can't move very well," Nancy said as she came out from behind the change wall.

"And these shoes!" Sam complained. "I think I might never walk again."

"It could be much worse you know." The professor stood admiring the transformed cousins. "The clothes you picked were those of the working middle class. Had you needed to be attired in upper class clothing, Nancy would have worn a large petticoat and a corset to cinch her waist in. There could have been little room for running! And you, Master Sam, would have had a large ruffled collar that wrapped around your neck in a circle, and a large hat would have graced your head!"

"Well, at least we'll fit in with the period of time," Nancy said, itching a bit at the rough cotton fabric.

"Yeah, Nike shoes and Levi jeans would have stood out a bit," Sam joked.

"You must go now. Be careful and Godspeed." The professor stepped back.

Holding Nancy's hand, Sam fit the triangle wedge to complete the coin. In what seemed to be an explosion, they were caught up in a spinning wheel with colours like a kaleidoscope flashing blue, red, green, and yellow. The noise in the air was like a dozen jet engines, and they felt as if they were spinning uncontrollably, just like you would be if you were being tumbled by a wave, but they weren't afraid. Although lasting only seconds, the cousins felt the sensation was going on for hours until all at once they tumbled onto a grassy knoll.

"Are you all right?" Nancy asked as she shook her dark curls to get the cobwebs out of her head.

"Fine, I think." Sam groaned. "You?"

"Yeah, all in one piece," Nancy said. "Where are we?"

The cousins were looking out over a wide river teeming with sailing vessels of all sizes and types. On the shore they could see people fishing, some with nets, and others with poles. In the background was a small city, with prominent church spires piercing the blue sky. The neatly attached buildings that made up the city were topped with red and black tile roofs and were tall and thin, each with a unique private garden in the rear. Cobblestone streets were filled with carts and wagons being pulled by oxen or horses and, in some cases, men. Loaded on the wagons were all types of goods, foods, and assorted commodities. Everywhere shops and open markets were bustling with merchants selling and people buying; others were engaged in conversation, and still others were travelling to attend to business. It was clearly a prosperous city.

"I believe we're in seventeenth-century Holland." Nancy spoke quietly as she took in the scene before her.

"And this must be Amsterdam," Sam said.

"We really did go back in time," Nancy said in awe. "And now we have to find the truth about Patron Van Eck and what happened to him and Jonathan."

"And Anna," Sam reminded Nancy.

"Yes, and Anna."

"Hold on, Sam." Nancy placed her hand on Sam's arm to slow him down. "We need a plan, and we need it fast, because we have company."

CHAPTER 4

Hans De Bruin was on his way into the city. He lived in a small village several miles from Amsterdam with his wife and daughter. A tailor by trade, he'd been commissioned to make a suit for his wealthy patron and was on his way to deliver it. He was riding a low wooden cart pulled by a team of oxen, and as he moved along the well worn cart path that led into the city, he let the cattle lead the way and his mind to wander. Today he would make a good profit and would be able to buy that special ring his wife had so admired. He would have loved to buy her whatever she desired, and she loved gold. It was warm out, and the rhythmic rocking of the cart had begun to lull him to sleep.

"Good day, sir!" Sam's voice rang out.

Hans was so startled he nearly fell out of the cart! As his eyes focussed on the strangers before him, he cried out, "Oh no, robbers!"

"We mean you no harm! We're not robbers," Nancy said.

Hans looked warily at the teenagers. "If you mean me no harm, what can I help you with?"

"We have come a long way. Can we share your cart and ride with you into the city?" Sam hoped they could have a ride because the shoes they had selected were so uncomfortable.

"Well then, I'm off to conduct some business. Climb aboard and I'll give you transportation to the city."

On the way to town, Nancy asked Hans why he was going into the city.

"It's best not to pry into others' business until you have stated your own." Hans sounded stern, but his eyes twinkled. He urged the cattle forward and they rode in silence for a while.

"I'm sorry," Nancy said quickly. "I didn't mean to pry. We're looking for Patron Van Eck. Do you know of him and where we might find him?"

"Van Eck! Yes, I know him. That's why I'm going to the city today. I'm a tailor by trade, and the patron is a merchant who has ordered some clothes from me. Why are you looking for him?"

"We were hoping to gain employment and were told he could help us." Sam spoke this hoping he sounded important.

After a few moments, Hans answered. "Van Eck could indeed help you find employment but let me tell you this. He is a shrewd man and one you must be careful around. Be careful how you approach him, for many have been brought to ruin at his hands."

"Thank you for the warning; we didn't know that," Nancy cautiously acknowledged.

"Where will you stay? We're going to be entering the city soon."

"We're new here and have no place in mind," Sam said.

The trio rode in silence as they continued into the city. All around them were the sounds of people calling back and forth, merchants crying out the name of their goods: "Bread for sale!" "Fish for you!" "Flowers!" the merchants called out in loud voices, determined to draw attention from the crowds walking and riding past. Storefront shops offered their wares in windows and on the street. Butcher shops hung beef on hooks in their windows; furniture stores had beautiful chairs and tables on display. Pottery shops had beautiful blue and white pieces of delft pottery on shelves in the stores. Finally, Hans stopped in front of a shop displaying dresses and men's suits.

"This is where I will stop," Hans said. "I have business today with Patron Van Eck. Come back here at 5:00 p.m.

today and I'll take you back to my farm for food and lodging tonight. Perhaps I'll be able to introduce you to the patron."

Sam and Nancy were surprised and thanked Hans after promising to be back at 5:00 p.m. sharp.

"Phew, that was a close one," Nancy said when they were alone. "What do you make of his warnings about Van Eck?"

"I think we take it seriously," said Sam. "It seems he can't be trusted"

"Agreed! Let's look around and get a feel for the city." Sam and Nancy walked away from the tailor's shop. In the window, a man looked on after them, a hard, piercing look of suspicion on his face. Sam looked back and their eyes met. Sam knew immediately it was Van Eck, and he didn't like what he saw.

It was twilight and the first stars of the night were beginning to twinkle when Hans returned. As they climbed aboard the wagon, they noticed he looked sullen and angry, so they stayed quiet, afraid to upset him. They rode along without speaking for about an hour. As they crested the hill, they saw below them flickering lights and guessed it was the village where the De Bruins lived. The ox pulling the cart sensed his warm stall and fresh hay were near and picked up his pace, as he realized his day of work would soon be over. The cart stopped in front of a wood and stone cottage set on a small plot of land. The cottage was painted white. To the left of the cottage stood a small unpainted barn-like structure to which Hans was leading the oxen to for the night. The flagstone path leading to a blue front door from the cobblestone street wound past a manicured flowerbed and herb garden, and the windows to either side of the door had shutters that were also painted blue. A small square window above the door suggested an upper floor to the cottage. In the back was a large vegetable garden.

Hans nodded to the barn. "You may rest in there. I'll bring you some food." With that, he went indoors.

The cousins made their way to the barn. Looking around, they noticed straw was readily available and seemed to invite them to sit. They hadn't been there very long when the door opened and a woman came in. Anika De Bruin stood a little over five feet tall. Her dark hair was braided and pinned to her lace cap. The black dress was accented ever so modestly with a small amount of lace, and her leather shoes were well worn. She was unsmiling and her blue eyes were piercing the faces of the two teenagers looking back at her. In her hands she held a tray with bowls of cabbage soup and a stack of thick black bread covered in butter and honey. The spoons were made of tin and the bowls of wood. There was a pitcher of ale and two small mugs to drink from.

"My husband has a big heart. I am not so generous with strangers. Just how do you plan to pay for your food and lodging?"

"Will this do?" Nancy asked as she held out her hand to Anika

The small gold nugget glowed in the light. Anika's eyes briefly flashed as she saw the gold, and then they hardened. Sam held his breath. Anika reached out, took the nugget, and bit it. Having satisfied herself it was real, she nodded to Nancy.

"This will cover one week's board and the food." Without another word, she turned and left, but Sam and Nancy both saw a thin cruel smile cross her lips.

"The professor said the gold might come in handy!"

"Boy, was he right."

The cousins tucked into the food, as they hadn't eaten during the day and were ravenous. Hearty and delicious, they licked the bowls clean, and not a crumb of the thick rye bread was left behind. With the meal ended, Sam lay down in the straw, and Nancy began to sing softly. Sam smiled as he remembered the song.

"I haven't heard that for a while; my grandmother used to sing it to me before I fell asleep."

"It's a song from both our families." Nancy paused in her singing. "I had it sung to me whenever I was anxious or afraid, and now I remember it."

"I was told it had been passed down through many generations and is supposed to have great power." Sam said this with a faraway look in his eyes. "Makes me a little drowsy, though, but we have much more work to be done."

"Yes, no time for sleeping on the job," Nancy agreed. "We need to listen in to Hans and Anika to learn more about Patron Van Eck."

"I agree," Sam replied. "In time we may have to use all of our special powers to solve this mystery."

CHAPTER 5

THE COUSINS ROSE AND crept to the cottage. Being careful not to be seen, they looked in the window. The cottage was clean and sparsely furnished. At the end of the room, a large fireplace served to both heat the room and provide fire to cook the meals. Some embroidered artwork graced the walls, and oil lamps provided light. Hans and Anika were deep in conversation.

"But how could Van Eck have taken advantage of you so?" Anika was demanding.

"He simply took the clothes I had crafted for him and claimed they weren't to his standard, so he would only pay half of what we'd agreed upon." Hans bitterly replied. "I had no choice but to sell them to him, for he threatened to blacklist me to the merchant's guild if I didn't agree."

"He is an evil man." Anika spat the words out. "One day, we will rise up and be his better. Still, our fortune seems to have come in the door with you. Imagine, a gold nugget for some room and board from the strangers."

"Yes, this was good fortune. But we must keep the newcomers hidden, as townsfolk will not take kindly to strangers."

"We will keep them here and see if there is more gold to be had." Anika allowed her lips to tighten in a thin smile.

"You know I don't approve of this." Hans frowned. "Let the strangers be; they seem harmless enough."

Anika spat out, "I will take their gold if they have more and turn them over to the king's guard."

Nancy and Sam had heard enough.

"She is horrible," Nancy said.

"We need to be wary of that one," Sam said. Nancy nodded and they quietly crept back to the barn.

At dawn, the village was already active. Cows were milked, eggs from chickens and ducks had been collected, and the wonderful smell of fresh baking drifted in the air. But in the barn, something far more serious was about to happen. The cousins were ready for Hans and Anika.

Anika entered the barn carrying a plate of pastries, eggs, and steaming coffee. She set them down on a barrel and prepared to leave when Nancy began to sing very softly. Surprised, Anika turned around to look at the girl. Nancy was looking directly into Anika's eyes with a piercing glare; her right hand was extended, and her body was slightly bent forward. Anika now stood perfectly still and began to sway. She was suddenly so drowsy she fell into the hay in a deep sleep.

"Quickly now," said Sam, "the sleep won't last that long, and I need to deal with Hans."

"Right," Nancy replied.

Moving quickly to the cottage, Sam spied motion in the back garden.

"There he is!" Sam crept into the back yard. Hans was just bending down over a small plant and was digging something out of the ground when Sam and Nancy came into view. Hans smiled sheepishly at the cousins as Nancy began to sing. The words and melody were so soft and soothing. Hans felt his body beginning to sway. He couldn't move and soon was snoring peacefully in his garden!

"Time to travel ahead ten years before Hans and Anika return to this present time. We still have a mystery to solve."

Grasping Sam's hand, Nancy reached down to take hold of the coin around her neck. Anika was starting to awaken.

"Hurry!" Sam said.

Nancy held the coin out to Sam, who placed the triangle into the coin. For a split second, the air was sucked into a vacuum. The cousins vanished.

Anika rose from her sleep. "Strange," she muttered. "Why am I bringing a tray of coffee and pastry to the barn? I must have been sleepwalking!"

Hans joined his wife in the barn. "I've been in a deep sleep dreaming about two strangers."

"I had the same dream. Why am I in the barn with coffee? Look!" Annika gasped. "Look at what I found under the hay." Holding out her hand, the gold nugget glowed.

"Anika, I must show you what I found in the garden. He held out his hand, and the trident glowed a rich sea green. It was truly mesmerizing. Hans began to feel the jewel wooing him. The power of the jewel began to awaken a sense of hope he hadn't felt before.

"We must dig further; there may be more!" Hans said as he grabbed a shovel and began to dig, Soon he would be richer than he'd ever dreamed. As he dug around his garden, he came across a beautiful coin. The etching on the coin looked like the etching on the trident. As he gazed upon his prize, he felt an odd sensation, as if his mind was being changed. Instead of feeling humble and at the mercy of those in power, he felt somehow empowered. Although he didn't understand the feeling, he felt that he could accomplish anything he put his mind to. Somehow, he knew his fortunes had changed forever. And indeed, they had.

The cousins again found themselves spinning out of control. The light flashed in multi colours, and they felt a pressure from inside their bodies similar to when too many friends pile on in a giant pillow fight. Suddenly, they landed in the same field where they'd started … but now it was ten years later.

"Here we go again." Sam seemed brighter. "And properly dressed!"

"That's right. And the year is 1633, also known as the Golden Age of Holland."

Sam looked at Nancy with some relief in his eyes. The secret of their special power was still between them.

"Let's go into the city and find a room and some food at an inn," Sam suggested.

"Did you know, Sam, that the Dutch refer to an inn as a *kroeg*?"

"No, I didn't know that, but when we were in Amsterdam, I saw one called the Golden Dragon."

"Sounds like a destination, Sam. Time to travel and find us a place to stay!"

CHAPTER 6

*H*ANS SAT IN THE living room of his townhouse. Fifteen years earlier, he had moved north and had bought a cottage on an acre of land just outside of Amsterdam. On his acre was the most remarkable find he could have ever dreamed of, a set of jewels that he and Anika had found and hidden, and a gold nugget that suddenly appeared. The couple's good fortune and wealth continued to grow at an astonishing rate. It seemed that whatever he put his hand to in agriculture or trade, prospered. Soon he became one of Amsterdam's leading business merchants. His family flourished and grew. Hans was proud of all his children but had a special place in his heart for Anna, his firstborn.

The city had continued to grow, and Hans had built a magnificent three-storey home on a site with canal access. Like all homes in Amsterdam, his was tall and narrow, being forty feet wide and sixty feet deep. The exterior was painted blue with white trim. The roof line had a marble crest depicting a lion on a shield held by two noblemen. The interior was gorgeous with imported wood adorning the stairwell, and plaster coving accenting the hall. Hans wasn't only prosperous, but he was also honest and likeable; consequently, he didn't have many seeking his ruin, so his clothing business grew and grew. He did have one enemy, though—Patron Van Eck, and not a day went by when the patron didn't plot to destroy him.

The year 1633 had ended badly for Hans. He still couldn't believe how he'd been so deceived by his enemy, Patron Van Eck. The contract to supply uniforms to a large hospital had seemed so secure. Hans had bought one hundred guilders worth of cloth fabric to make the uniforms—more than two years' wages for an average working man. He had borrowed the money from the bank owned by Van Eck and had pledged his house as security for the loan. He'd spent months sewing the uniforms, and on the day of delivery discovered that Van Eck had convinced the hospital board to refuse the delivery. Hans let his mind replay the confrontation:

"But you have to accept them. We have a contract!" Hans was livid.

"We have no contract." Van Eck's rat-like face was curled in a sneer.

"Here it is!" Hans produced a document and shook it at Van Eck.

"Look again at the signatures; you have no witness," mocked Van Eck. "And you owe my bank the money. Pay me in seventy-two hours or I'll seize your house."

"But how can I sell so many hospital uniforms in just three days? You know what you ask is impossible. You've wanted my house for years, and now you aim to take it by trickery! Never! I will see you dead first." Hans stormed through the tavern door, followed by Van Eck's mocking laughter.

Sam and Nancy had observed the fight from their table in the corner.

"This is a terrible thing." Nancy's concern was evident. "Do you think we should help him?"

Sam looked at Nancy and shook his head in a warning motion. "Not so fast, Nancy," Sam warned. "Let's follow Hans and see if we can find out how this plays out. He has prospered so much he must have found the magic jewels, and we still have to get close enough to him to find them."

Without another word, the cousins rose and left the tavern. Hans wouldn't know he was being followed, but someone was watching the cousins from the shadows of the tavern and slipped out behind them.

"What's the matter?" Hans was brought back from his thoughts by Anika: "When you left for your meeting with Van Eck, you were in such high spirits."

"We're facing ruin, Anika. Everything we own could be lost." Hans buried his head in his hands as he said this.

"How? Why?" Anika asked, alarm rising in her voice. As Hans told the story, Anika's face began to harden. "I have an idea, Hans. Last week when I was in the market, I met Mrs. Van Hoff. Do you remember Jos Van Hoff, her husband? He's involved in a new export business. Go and see him; maybe he can help."

Hans walked quickly and with purpose as he made his way to the business district of Amsterdam. His anger was still burning as he thought about his plight. *Surely Van Eck will pay for this one day*, he thought. But for now, he needed to sell his merchandise.

As he walked along the street, the sights and sounds of Amsterdam surrounded him. Seventeenth-century

Amsterdam was an exciting place to live. Narrow three-storey buildings flanked the multiple canals that ran throughout the city. Painted in every colour imaginable, the stone and brick homes all had distinctive roof tops, some of which reminded Hans of a set of steps running up to a landing and then running back down again, while others had semi-circle arches on top. Most of the houses were so narrow that furniture couldn't be carried up the stairs, so a large hook on the roof top had been installed to hoist goods to the floors above the street. Most of the houses also doubled as warehouse and manufacturing centres with the living quarters on the top floor. In front and behind the houses were the canals, where many small boats filled with every type of product imaginable moved effortlessly through the water.

Alongside the canals, the cobblestone street was teeming with wagons headed for the central marketplace. Horse-drawn carriages carried wealthy passengers to their destinations, and many pedestrians crowded the sidewalks. Women were dressed in beautiful dresses that almost touched the ground. The lace and embroidered bodices were accented by beautiful wool shawls. Lace caps were common as were the dark soft leather shoes. Men were proudly attired in black coats adorned at the neck by large ruffled collars, their silk stockings prominent above the large buckles on their shoes. Large top hats with wide brims completed their attire.

In the middle of this show of wealth and prosperity, Hans looked the part, but he knew that if he couldn't trade his clothing for a profit, he would be cast onto the street— penniless, homeless, and without hope. Oh, how he hated Patron Van Eck!

Hans arrived at his destination, the office of the Dutch East India Company, where he hoped to meet Jos Van Hoff, a merchant doing business with the company. The building itself was only twenty feet wide, but was one hundred feet deep and went all the way to a canal at the back. The colour was blue with white trim. At the roof peak (right between the two sets of imaginary stairs), was a beautiful red shield with a yellow dragon emblazoned on it. Two soldiers made of plaster stood to either side. The entry door was carved oak, rounded at the top, and painted black. Three stone stairs led up to the landing. Hans took a deep breath and entered along with three other people he didn't know.

"What is your business here?" The doorman spoke from behind an office window, which was in an alcove to the right of the door. He didn't look up.

"I'm here to speak with Jos Van Hoff."

"Oh yes, of course, Herr De Bruin. I'm sorry I didn't recognize you immediately. You'll find him on the trading floor. Last door at the end of the hall."

"Thank you." Hans started down the hallway. To his left was a stairway going up to the floors above. Partway along the hallway were several doors opening into offices where merchants were trading among each other. The ceilings were covered in white plaster carving that resembled rope that looped gracefully along the deep blue walls. Trim and doors were painted white, and the dark oak floors were worn in the middle. The cousins, who had been following Hans, had slipped in behind him. He glanced at them briefly, and a puzzled look came on his face.

"Do I know you?" he asked. "You seem so familiar."

"No, sir, unless it was at the market sometime," Sam answered.

"Strange, I could have sworn I knew them." Hans muttered as he walked away.

"And what is your business here?" The question was directed to the cousins.

"We're here to ask if we might find work." Sam spoke confidently, knowing that teenagers were considered adults in the seventeenth century. All the while Nancy kept her eye on Hans, knowing they had to get into the room with him and Van Hoff.

"Go to the warehouse on the dock; they might have something." The doorman tipped his head toward the hallway. "Follow that way to the dock."

Sam and Nancy quickly followed Hans. Looking back, they noticed the doorman wasn't watching them.

"Quick, in here!" Sam hissed and pointed to a door beside the room Hans had just entered.

The cousins found themselves in another meeting room. There was a window on the wall that opened onto an alleyway filled with lumber and wooden barrels. Climbing out of the window, they negotiated the stacks of wood until they were directly below the window of the room where Hans was. Cautiously they peeked into the room. They could make out Hans speaking to a round figure with an enormous head of white hair. He was seated at a desk, his wire-framed spectacles glinting in the light, but his piercing blue eyes showed he could be ruthless.

"And just how many hospital uniforms did you make?" Van Hoff was asking Hans.

"Over one hundred, and now I have no place to sell them."

"Oh, that is not so. At the Dutch East India Company, we have supplied hospitals in England with equipment many times, as well as markets all over Europe and even Africa! We'll find a buyer."

"But, sir, how long will it take? Patron Van Eck is demanding his money."

"Van Eck!" Van Hoff rose to his feet. "I didn't realize *he* was involved. I have no use for him and will have no business dealings with that scoundrel."

"No, sir, you don't understand," Hans pleaded. "It is I who was deceived by Van Eck and now stand to lose everything."

"He is indeed a harsh man. I'd like to teach him a lesson. I myself will buy your goods. I've heard of your work and believe it is sound. I need to make profit for myself but will give you a fair price."

"And where will you send the uniforms to?"

"I'm the district regent," replied Van Hoff. "I've thought of forming a hospital for my people."

"I am so grateful." Hans was humbled and moved to tears.

"Come now," said Van Hoff, "Let me give you a glass of port wine and talk terms for the purchase. I will not stand by and let Van Eck ruin another good man."

All at once there was a great crash from outside the room. Sam had lost his footing because of his slippery shoes and fallen off the barrel he was standing on, taking Nancy down with him. Sam and Nancy quickly untangled themselves and ran to the dock. Casting around, they realized they were trapped by the canal.

"What is your business here?" Van Hoff shouted out of the window. "Somebody grab those two spies!"

Desperately, the cousins looked around. Sam realized Van Hoff had gone inside his building as he headed for the door and that for a few seconds nobody could see them.

"Quick, over here is a boat!" Sam jumped onboard and was lifting a tarp. Nancy dove in behind him, although her dress was slowing her down. Just in time, they were hidden, as they heard voices.

"They were spies; we must find them." Van Hoff was yelling to the dockworkers.

"These are dangerous times with spies and thieves everywhere. I can't see them, but this is what they look like."

Hidden under the tarp, Sam and Nancy heard their description being clearly given to the men on the dock.

"He's about six feet tall with blond hair and an athletic build. He's wearing tan britches and a black coat. She's slim, about five feet six inches, dark curly hair, and wearing a blue dress. If you find them, you know what to do."

"Aye aye, sir."

The minutes seemed to drag. The hidden teens heard footsteps on the ship's deck. Sounds of ropes being undone and stowed away were followed by a gentle rocking. The boat was moving! Peeking out from the tarp, the cousins could see the land slowly slipping away. The rocking of the boat increased as it picked up speed. The smell of the water was salty, and the breeze from the shore would have been refreshing were it not for the anxiety beginning to rise in the cousins. Footsteps on the deck nearby caused the cousins to duck for cover.

"Who secured that tarp?" bellowed the captain.

"I was sure it was tied down, Skipper," the first mate replied.

"Tie it down now then before it blows away."

"Aye, sir."

Sam and Nancy heard the ropes being pulled across the tarp and suddenly felt the tarp tightening over them. They were trapped!

CHAPTER 7

JAKE VAN ECK STOOD in the shadows as he watched the supply barge leave the dock. In fact, he had been shadowing the cousins the whole time. Jake was gifted with the ability to blend unseen into any room. He had learned of his gifting when he was ten and hiding from his parents. Since then, he'd spent many hours spying on people. At first it was just fun, but one day he'd been discovered by a master spy. He smiled as he remembered being thirteen years old.

"Hey, Jake, can I see you after school?" The most beautiful girl Jake had ever seen was talking to him!

"Sure, Mary-Ann." Jake was all tongue-tied and felt hot. "How about a Coke at Jimmy's?"

"That sounds great; you can walk me there after school today."

All the rest of that day Jake couldn't wait until the bell rang. He met Mary-Ann Turncoat and together they walked to the favourite coffee shop. Finding a booth, they sat down.

"Jake," she began, "there's someone I'd like you to meet."

The older teen who joined them was from Timespan High, and Jake knew him by reputation and was flattered to be in his company.

"Jake," he began, "good to meet you. Do you know who I am?"

"Yeah, I know who you are ... you're Mike, but"—he looked at Mary-Ann—"why are you here?"

"I've been watching you and am very impressed with your ability to spy!"

"You know?" Jake was shocked.

"Oh yes, we know. We *all* know!" Both Mike and Mary-Ann grinned, and Jake knew he belonged!

His first task had been to spy on teachers and students and find enough dirt on them to allow the master spy, a man he'd never met but feared all the same, to blackmail them. Jake was very good at this and enjoyed it. Over time, his main task was to keep an eye out for the one who would be wearing the magic coin. It was a task he took very seriously, and he'd attended to it diligently. When Nancy walked into Timespan High, he knew he'd found his mark and immediately started planning how to steal the coin. The power he could wield by going back to change history to suit himself boggled his evil mind. The problem was her meddlesome cousin. He tried to break his ankle by tripping him. When that didn't work, he tried to scare him off the professor. That didn't work either and now here he was in Holland having slipped into the time travel orbit by being a shadow when the cousins moved around time. Yes, he'd been in the barn, and in the tavern, and at the docks, but had been unable to catch them.

"I can't see them anywhere," said Hans. "They did look a bit familiar to me, though."

"No matter," said Van Hoff. "I'll post some extra guards. Come inside again; we have work to do and one hundred uniforms to load onto this barge. The ship sets sail for England in the morning."

As the men returned to the office, Jake grinned a wolfish grin. *Of course I'll follow my ancestor Patron Van Eck*, he thought. *He'll find Hans De Bruin and lead me back to the cousins, and then the coin and the jewels will be mine.* He'd heard everything the professor had said, and he knew of the mission. With that, he melted back into the shadows, where he could keep an eye on Hans.

"What do you mean the loan has been repaid!" Van Eck raged at his bank manager.

"Hans came in today and paid it in full." The manager cringed as he said it.

"I must know how he got the money!" Van Eck shouted as he stormed out of his bank. "Out of my way," he bellowed as he strode down the main street leading to the Dutch East India Company. All the way he kept fuming about how his plans to steal De Bruin's house and ruin Hans had been foiled.

Vowing to get even, he stormed into the Dutch East India Company office.

Formed in 1602, the company became a large merchant group and enabled many to grow wealthy, either by using the resources to buy and sell merchandise, which was the intent of the group, or by share ownership and profiting from the rise in stock price (this was the first company in the world to offer shares to the public). Van Eck, a devious man, had been able to lie and cheat others of their money and had invested in shares of the trading company when they were first offered. During the subsequent rise in value, he'd persuaded gullible but trusting merchants to let him be the middleman in their dealings with the DEIC in exchange for even more shares. Over several years, he had amassed a fortune in shares and had bought a bank and a mill and had control over several large ships. He was powerful and was used to getting what he wanted, and he wanted Hans' house. He had also wanted to marry Anika, for they were well suited, but that too had been denied him, so his vengeful state had simmered for years. He hated Hans De Bruin and daily plotted ways to destroy him.

"Where is he?" Van Eck's fury caught the doorman by no surprise.

"On the dock; go look for yourself." The doorman went back to reading the newspaper.

Van Eck stormed down the hall and onto the dock, where he found Van Hoff supervising the loading of a shipment of goods. Van Eck's eyes narrowed, his jaw tightened, and his body tensed as he sized up his prey. Had he been a cobra he would have fanned his neck and reared back before he spat the venom of his words.

"Where are my goods?" Van Eck demanded.

"What goods would those be?" came Van Hoff's calm reply.

"My hospital uniforms. What have you done with them?"

"I bought them at a fair price and am shipping them out."

"You can't have bought them; I have a contract." Van Eck waved the paper in front of Van Hoff.

"You mean the same one that wasn't witnessed?" Hans mocked.

"I'll have you banned from the company and see you ruined." Van Eck was wild-eyed with rage.

"You have no legal charge, Van Eck. The goods are paid for in full and on that boat heading to market."

Looking down the canal, Van Eck caught sight of a barge rounding the corner. The vessel was indeed loaded with goods heading to a larger ship in the harbour and from there out to England. He glared at Van Hoff and stalked away. From under the tarp the cousins breathed a sigh of relief as they peeked out and recognized the figure of Van Eck growing smaller and smaller.

"That was close," breathed Nancy.

"Yeah, but how do we get off this barge?"

"Not sure of that one, Sam. We need a plan, and we need it fast because I have a feeling stowaways aren't real popular."

As the boat picked up speed, the cousins began to worry.

Amsterdam in the seventeenth century was a centre of commerce. The harbour had been created by building a dam to stop the Amstel River from flowing into the sea. To prevent flooding, the dam could open and allow the river to continue to flow. This ingenious engineering masterpiece, combined with the natural business sense of the Dutch, created a wealth that allowed the Dutch to become a superpower. The Dutch built ocean going ships, known as a *fluyt*, which remained anchored while they awaited the smaller vessels that had been loaded with goods from the city to approach them. When the captain of the *fluyt* was sure the goods were correct, he allowed them to be loaded.

"Undo that tarp; we may have to show the goods," the captain commanded.

"Aye, sir." The deckhands began untying the ropes holding the tarp down.

Under the tarp, the cousins held their breath and remained motionless as they heard the ropes hit the deck.

"What is your business here?" the *fluyt*'s captain called down.

"We come from the Dutch East India dock with goods of cloth and hospital uniforms."

"I know nothing of that! I am expecting pottery and furniture!"

"That is not what we have!"

"Then be on your way. I have no need to see your goods."

"Where do we go now, Skipper?" one of the mates asked.

"Back to the dock to get the name of the right ship to deliver to. Always a foul up when Van Hoff is in a rush."

"We won't be at the dock until nightfall now. We'll have to find our new ship in the morning, and you can be sure there will be cussing and shouting when we return."

"Not from us there won't be," Sam whispered.

The snoring of the guard who was assigned to watch the vessel was deep and rhythmic. Shivering under the tarp, the cousins were freezing cold and had been huddled together for warmth for hours.

"I think it's safe to go now." Sam spoke between clenched teeth to keep them from chattering.

"I can't see a thing," Nancy said as she peered out from under the tarp into the gloom.

"Just follow close to me Nancy and watch you don't trip on something."

The cousins moved forward, carefully picking their way across the deck, every sound magnified in the still night air.

"I can just make out the gangplank ahead, Nancy. Can you hurry up?" Sam whispered this but to Nancy he seemed to be shouting.

"This dress I'm in doesn't make it easy, Sam. It makes me so clumsy; I hate it!"

"At least the clothes are black, but these shoes weigh a ton." Sam said this as he was starting down the gangway and had taken his shoes off to walk more quietly.

"Time to be careful now, Nancy. We don't want to wake the guard up."

"As if I don't know that!" Nancy muttered under her breath.

The cousins, creeping down the dock, had just passed the guard. Sam put his shoes back on because the planks on the docks were rough underfoot and the sound of his heels making a hollow clicking sound seemed to fill the air. Nancy's dress rustled as she moved, and she was convinced the whole city would awaken.

"I think we're making enough noise to wake the dead," Sam breathed.

"But not the guard," Nancy replied with a slight smile as she started to sing. "Holland is famous for beer, and I suspect our guard is a good customer, but the magic will have him sleep like a baby."

"Just have to make it past the office building now and we can get back to the tavern." Sam had just said that when they heard voices coming right at them from around the corner. Looking wildly about, the cousins realized they had nowhere to hide. They were trapped!

"I heard there were a couple of thieves about today." The dock worker was smoking a pipe as he spoke to his friend.

"Got away they did. I heard Van Hoff and De Bruin had a shipment heading out to England that the thieves might have been after. Turns out the wrong shipment went out … just uniforms!"

"Ha ha, some thief would look good in a nurse's uniform now, wouldn't he?"

"Yeah, real cute."

The two dockhands passed by a couple locked in an embrace.

"Maybe they're the spies," one of the dockhands joked.

"If they are, you'd think they could find some other dock to mess around on, wouldn't you?" The two walked on, laughing at what they had just passed by.

"Okay, enough of that," Nancy said as she pushed Sam away. "A bit too close for comfort."

"Yeah, in more ways than one! Let's get out of here." Sam said this as he and Nancy hurried back to their room at the Golden Dragon.

CHAPTER 8

"So that's how we managed to survive, my dear Anika." Hans was relaxing in his study.

"I'm so pleased. And you're in good standing with the merchant guild?"

"Very good. In fact, they're most interested in my contribution to the company. I should be able to add many new items to the next shipment to England."

"It seems our good fortune is following us, despite Van Eck."

"I don't ever want to hear that man's name spoken again." Hans briefly tightened his grip on the jewels on his watch chain and soon felt much better.

"No, never again," agreed Anika, brightening up and changing the subject. "You know, soon we will be presenting our Anna to society balls. We already have many invitations. We must find a way to marry her well."

"Yes, I guess this is so, but it seems so soon to lose my lovely Anna."

Anna De Bruin sat beside her upstairs window looking out onto the street. At fifteen, she was a beautiful young woman. Her blonde curls framed her face in such a way that could only be described as captivating. Her blue eyes were the colour of a summer sky at noon, and her fine bone structure suggested royalty. She was her father's pride and joy… and she knew it! A pebble made a loud *ting* against her window, disturbing her thoughts.

"Jonathan, my love, what are you doing?" Opening her window, she spoke softly to the young man below.

"I had to see you, Anna!" the young man standing beneath the oil burning street lantern called back.

"If Father sees you, there will be trouble." But her voice betrayed her pleasure in this most welcome interruption.

The handsome young man with dark curls looked up at Anna's window.

"When can I meet you, Anna?"

"Tomorrow I will be going to the market. Meet me in front of the Galleon Cafe at noon; I'll try to slip away from Mother."

"I'll be there."

But they would not be alone. There was someone, or something, in the shadows watching and listening.

Jonathan Van Eck was seated in front of the Galleon Cafe in the Muntplein Square sipping his coffee as the town clock, which was known as the Mint Tower, chimed twelve times. The square was overlooking the busy Amstel River. Ordinarily, Jonathan, who was heir to the Van Eck shipping empire, would be taking an interest in which ships were sailing past. Today he had eyes for only one thing: Anna! She was shopping with her mother and was close by. She had looked his way and smiled at him for a moment. He held his breath as he waited for her to pass by.

"Mother, I'm tired," Anna said. "Can we stop at this cafe for a rest?"

"Honestly, child, we just left our house not thirty minutes ago. How can you be tired already? We have to buy shoes and some lace for your new gown and have no time for a rest."

Seated beside Jonathan in an adjacent table, Sam and Nancy were listening. They could see that the handsome young man hadn't taken his eyes off Anna, but that was to be expected. What was not expected was what happened next. From out of nowhere, a figure rushed by, upsetting their table and spilling the food and drink everywhere! Jonathan leaped out of the way and crashed into Anna, just managing to catch her before she fell.

"Watch out, you fool!" Jonathan called to the figure, who was already vanishing into the crowd.

"Are you harmed?" The question to Anna was spoken quietly.

"No, quite all right."

"Here, take my seat." Turning to Anna's mother, he said, "Your daughter appears quite shaken; she should rest."

Flustered, Anika replied, "I'll go for a carriage to return home immediately."

"I'll stay with her while you go, madam. She'll be quite safe."

"I will return shortly; thank you, sir." Anika left in search of her carriage.

"We only have a few precious minutes, Anna," Jonathan said with a grin. "I don't know who that was, but if I did, I would thank him!"

"Jonathan, you know if either of our parents learn of our love, they'll never allow a marriage."

"I know, but maybe your father will change his mind."

"And would yours? They hate each other and want us to meet other people."

"This feud has gone on for too long. We have to find a way."

From the shadows, Jake allowed a tight-lipped grin to spread across his face as he thought, *And my fortunes would be so much better. I must get the trident and magic coin. If I can stop time, I can change the course of history and be rich!*

"Well, Sam, it seems those two have a destiny together. I wonder who the man is. He seems familiar somehow."

"Nancy, you romantic! Don't you recognize him? That's Jonathan Van Eck from the painting!"

"Of course!" Nancy exclaimed. "Now we know to follow him. We can find out what happened to him and Anna."

"Let's do that from the shadows," said Sam, shaking his hair from his eyes. "Our assignment is to find the hidden truth of the Van Eck and De Bruin feud, and we don't want to get caught."

"What makes you think there's something hidden, Sam?"

"Just something in that woman, Anika, that gives me the creeps. Such a nasty woman! She would do anything to advance her own social status … even murder."

"Yes, she and Van Eck are dangerous people and we must be careful!" Nancy shuddered. "Look, Anika has returned with a carriage. It sure seems that Anna and Jonathan are a perfect match They just seem to look so right together. We're still no closer to the De Bruin family and the jewels, but I have an idea."

"What is it?"

"Let's go back to the Golden Dragon and I'll tell you."

"It says here that Hans was the owner of a famous flame tulip that was named Anna Fierus." Nancy and Sam had returned to their room in the Golden Dragon, and Nancy was reading from the family history book. "You need to understand the curious and short-lived business bubble known as the Tulip Mania of 1635–1637, and I know just the way to teach you." Nancy wiggled her eyebrows at Sam as she said this.

"Oh boy, I know what that means." Sam shook his head and looked up at the ceiling. "Here we go again."

CHAPTER 9

THE ROOM RESERVED FOR buying and selling was filling up as Van Eck strode in to take a seat at his usual table. The year 1635 was ending, and a new form of commerce was taking the invited merchant class to a whole new level of prosperity. Tulip trading was all the rage, as the nobility had taken a fancy to the beautiful flowers after a merchant had imported the bulbs from Persian royalty. Owning specialty tulip bulbs was the new status symbol. The merchant class had new wealth and wanted the world to know it.

Not everyone was invited to take part in this buying and selling of tulip bulbs; only the elite in the city were so entitled. Each night, they would gather in the room and discuss business and politics. As the city grew, the power and status of these merchants grew as well. It was considered the height of success if you were part of this group, and keeping up status and appearance fuelled their proud egos. In order to gain a seat at the table, you had to be invited, which kept the participants down to a very tight group, as common folk just couldn't get in. The elite would buy and sell the tulip bulbs amongst each other, and some were even sold to royalty. As the popularity of the bulbs grew among the traders, the price of the bulb continued to go up and up. It was a fabulous business.

But that didn't mean there were only a few Dutchmen growing the bulbs. Many of the up-and-coming merchants were quite knowledgeable and skilled at growing the bulbs. It was the trading for profit that belonged to just a small percentage of the population, and it was to that group that Van Eck belonged and Anika wished Hans to be a part of.

"Van Hoff just stole my cargo from me." Van Eck was seething as he spoke to the merchants seated at his table.

"I heard he bought the goods fair and square … and stands to make a good profit too."

"Van Hoff is an honourable man from all of my dealings with him, as is De Bruin. Are you sure it wasn't you who was trying to steal the cargo?"

"Enough of this." Van Eck spat the words out. "I have money to make at tonight's tulip auction." He turned his back on the merchants at the table and didn't see the amused smirks on all of their faces.

"I have one deep red tulip for sale, a pedigree known as 'General Generals.' Am I bid ten guilders?" The auction had begun, and Van Eck raised his hand. It was common during the tulip mania to give the bulbs important sounding names, so names like 'General Generals,' or 'Imperial Star' were common among the sellers. There seemed no end in sight for the profit to be made trading tulips. Van Eck's eyes narrowed a bit as he thought for a minute of how he could crush that pest De Bruin. He would, he thought, and soon.

Hans stood in his back garden. It was May 15, 1636. He was inspecting a single tulip that was in bloom and quite stunning. The petals had come up in orange and red stripes. This was indeed the most desirable and rare of all tulips. *I shall name it 'Anna Fireus.'*

Hans's thoughts were interrupted by a shrill voice: "Who will you sell this to?" Anika had appeared beside him.

"I don't know; I'm not a member of the merchant exchange. Besides, if I sell the bulb, I'll receive payment only once. But what if I can reproduce it? Then I could sell it again!"

"But whoever you sell it to could also do the same, driving the price down at the same time."

"It's so beautiful. I am going to offer it to Van Hoff. If anyone deserves it, it's him."

"*Stephens*," Hans called to his servant.

"Yes, sir?" The shadowy figure of Jake appeared.

"Take this note to Van Hoff at the dock and bring me his reply."

Jake took the note and gave a small bow. As he headed to the dock, he was pleased with himself. He'd been hiding at the docks when he heard that Hans needed a servant. Getting hired had been easy. After all, every candidate Hans had intended to interview had mysteriously not showed up. Jake grinned to himself as he remembered tripping one into the canal and breaking the arm of another who didn't see the carriage coming because his hat had suddenly blown over his eyes. Only Jake made it to the interview, so he was hired. Now he was working close to De Bruin and could keep an eye on things and steal the jewels at an opportune moment.

"Sir, I have a letter for you from my master, Hans De Bruin." Jake was standing in the office of Van Hoff as he delivered the letter.

"Wait here while I read this." Van Hoff placed his wire framed glasses on the bridge of his long nose and sat down to read:

Mr. Jos Van Hoff
Dutch East India Company
May 15, 1636

My Dear Van Hoff,

I would very much appreciate your counsel in a matter of great importance. As you know, I have been engaged in the business of tulip growing for a few years now. For the most part, it has been a passion with its rewards. I understand there exists a network of merchants engaged in the buying and selling of the bulbs for profit.

I have just discovered one of my bulbs has a flower with flame petals. It is so rare, I must seek your advice on how I can sell it. Could you come today for supper?

Yours,

Hans De Bruin

Van Hoff sat down immediately and wrote back:

Mr. Hans De Bruin
1500 Vanderness St.
Amsterdam
May 15, 1636

My Dear Hans,

I will be delighted to come to supper tonight. One word of caution: say nothing of the flame tulip to anyone. I repeat, say nothing. I will come for 7:00 p.m.

Yours,

Jos Van Hoff.

"Take this reply to Master De Bruin immediately." He gave Jake a guilder. "This is to ensure speed!"

As Jake left the building, he had a slight detour in mind, for he had read the contents of the letter and knew of someone who would pay him well for this information.

"And you're sure the tulip had flame petals?" Van Eck was sitting in the corner of the Golden Dragon tavern.

"Quite sure, my Lord." Jake was standing in the shadows pretending to be afraid of Van Eck.

"And why would you betray De Bruin to me?"

"I heard you were a dealer of tulips and thought you would share the profit."

"Share the profit? You foolish man, I never share profit with anyone!"

"Even if it would result in getting the better of De Bruin?" Jake watched as Van Eck's scowl gradually turned to a thoughtful gaze.

"Yes, it could do that. All right, I'll pay you twenty guilders for information on the bulb Anna Fierus." Grabbing Jake's arm in a vice like grip he pulled him close. "But beware you don't cross me on this; your life is cheap." He gave a shove as he released him, causing Jake to fall to the ground. "Very cheap!"

"This is a rare flower indeed, Hans." Van Hoff was inspecting the bulb closely. "Such beautiful colours! It's a prize."

"How can I sell this when I'm not a member of the exchange?"

"There's a new and better way to do this." Van Hoff straightened up. "Let us go into your study while I explain this to you."

The two men went into the study, followed by Jake, who was carrying two glasses and a container of port wine.

"You may go now, Stephens," Hans said, dismissing Jake. "Now Jos, tell me of the new way to sell the bulb. I'm anxious to hear it, but you must assure me Van Eck will not hear of this."

"I am in no way anxious to enrich Van Eck," Jos said as he sipped his port.

Unnoticed by either of the two men, Jake had used his power to blend into the corner, where he stood so still, he looked like a shadow. He would hear and report everything to Van Eck.

"I'm going to introduce the merchants at the exchange to a new way to transact business by forming a stock exchange for the tulip trade." Van Hoff was seated by the fire and smoking a pipe. "Currently, one has to see the tulips and barter for the value. I propose to change all of that. Instead of handling the actual tulips, I'll sell shares for the right to own the tulips in the future. The owner of the shares may in turn sell those along to someone else for more or less than they paid. The value will be set by the buyer of the shares daily, and money for the shares will be settled at the end of the day by a treasurer at the exchange. I intend to call my business a stock exchange for tulips."

"That sounds brilliant." Hans sensed an excitement growing. "But how will you keep people honest about settling up at the end of the evening?"

"In order to attend the exchange, members will have to deposit sufficient funds with the exchange treasurer to cover the activities. Prior to each transaction, the exchange will have to approve the limit of spending. It will be up to the treasurer of the exchange to ensure that both the seller has a legal claim to the shares, and the buyer has sufficient funds to complete the purchase."

"You seem to have thought this through, Jos." Hans sensed that the breakthrough he had been hoping for was here.

"It gets better, because I've arranged with a number of merchants to create a bank for lending if buyers want to borrow to buy shares."

"I'd like to be a member of the exchange, if you'd sponsor me." Hans watched Jos for his reaction.

"I'll take you along tonight, but only to watch and learn; say nothing of Anna Fierus."

Jos and Hans entered the Golden Dragon tavern and proceeded to go upstairs to a large room that had been set aside for the merchants to trade their tulip bulbs. As was the evening custom, men were bartering for the tulips on display. Van Hoff stood and walked to the front of the room.

"Gentlemen, may I have your attention." And with that, he explained his new method of selling shares that guaranteed the buying and selling of tulips. The merchants in the room were all familiar with how a stock exchange worked. Jos Van Hoff was enabling his fellow merchants in the Tulip Trading Club to do the same for their tulip speculations. There was great excitement in the room as this new opportunity to enhance the speculation in tulip trading began to sink in.

"How soon can we participate in this?" called out a merchant.

"My exchange can start next week," Van Hoff answered.

"I'll be a part of this if Van Hoff is president," another chimed in.

The room resounded with a chorus of, "Hear, hear." And so the Tulip Trading Club formally was birthed.

Van Eck was in the room taking this in. The information Jake had slipped him was going to be useful. He began to scheme how he could take over the exchange and manipulate the trading. *Yes*, he thought, *this will be good for me and bad for De Bruin*. He allowed a slight smile to cross his lips.

"What about you, De Bruin? Have you nothing to sell tonight?" Van Eck was baiting Hans, hoping to get him to reveal his prize, Anna Fierus.

"What I have to sell is of greater value than you could ever hope to afford, but tonight I'm here as a guest of Van Hoff to watch the unveiling of the Tulip Trading Club."

Van Eck slowly rose to his feet, his face contorted into a mask of rage. His eyes grew large and his jaw tightened into an image of hate. Clenching his fists, he took a threatening step toward Hans.

"Don't rise up yet, Hans," Jos whispered as he placed a restraining hand on Hans' shoulder. "We have a long way to go before we can reel in the catch."

When Hans didn't move, Van Hoff called over to the young man and woman standing at the serving counter. "More wine for our table." Sam and Nancy hustled right over.

"It was easy to find work here tonight," Sam said under his breath to Nancy, "but all this makeup we're wearing to disguise ourselves is really uncomfortable."

"It is, but it should keep us from being recognized." Nancy said this as she was trying not to stare at Hans' pocket watch. "Do you see what's at the end of the chain?" she whispered to Sam.

"There they are!" Sam hissed under his breath. The trident and the coin were flashing their beautiful colours in the room's soft light. The greens and golds were calling to the cousins in a way that spoke of the mystery of the ages that the jewels were part of. "Now that we know where they are, we have to figure out a way to obtain them and bring them back to the professor."

"And that's not going to be easy. Look who the butler is!"

CHAPTER 10

At first, neither Sam nor Nancy could quite comprehend who they were seeing. Standing just outside of the door, Jake was waiting at the coach for Hans, a bored look on his face. It was like a nightmare for the cousins. They knew him from the school, but how did he arrive in seventeenth-century Amsterdam?

"How is *he* here?" Sam's face was hard.

"I don't know, but I have to know *what* he's doing here." Nancy had a determined look on her face.

"I knew he was trouble from the day I met him. If he blows our cover, we'll never get the jewels and learn the story of the Van Eck and De Bruin fortune."

"It's worse than that, Sam," said Nancy. "If he's working close to Hans, how will we ever get near the jewels?"

"And the other question is: How much does he know?" Sam mused.

As the cousins continued to serve the tables, they kept a wary eye on Jake, who still hadn't noticed that the cousins were serving the tables.

"We're going to have to make our move soon," Nancy said.

"Now that we have some competition, I agree." Sam said this knowing the danger of trying to steal the jewels right in public.

The auction was winding down and the merchants were making the final bids on the tulips when the cousins saw the opportunity to get the jewels.

"One last time, De Bruin," Van Eck jibed. "What do you have to sell?"

He said this is such a loud voice that the auctioneer heard it.

"Patron Van Eck, you know the rules; only members are allowed to buy and sell, and De Bruin is not a member."

"Then make him one!" thundered Van Eck. "I will even be the sponsor."

"I tell you, Van Eck, I have nothing to sell you!"

"What about Anna Fierus?"

"How do you know of her? You are a spy and a thief."

"How dare you!" Van Eck slapped Hans hard across the face.

At this, there was such an uproar that all the merchants jumped to their feet, yelling at each other. Beer and food were spilled everywhere, and tables were overturned. People started pushing and shoving, and Hans never noticed the small hand of a young woman slip inside his pocket and remove the jewels.

"We have it," Nancy breathed to Sam as they crawled across the floor to escape the brawl. "Let's get out of here while we can!"

"But how can we get past Jake on the door?" Sam said. "Can you sing him to sleep?"

"I'd have to put the entire room to sleep," Nancy responded. "Maybe he won't recognize us in our disguise."

Jake had responded to the brawl and was making his way into the room. By now the commotion had died down and the men were resuming their places. Hans stormed out of the room and Jake had to follow, but not before looking back at Sam and Nancy with a hard, angry glare.

"And that's how I came to have this welt across my face." Hans was having a glass of port wine and telling Anika of his evening.

"Do you think you'll be allowed to join the merchants' stock exchange and trade tulips?" Anika asked, thinking of nothing more than the status she might lose if her husband was denied the privilege of membership.

"Many were appalled at my treatment and were demanding Van Eck apologize," Hans said. "My guess is I'll be invited back. What I can't understand is how Van Eck knew of Anna Fierus."

"How many were aware of her?" Anika asked.

Hans stood up and walked to the fire. "Only our family and Van Hoff."

"Could Stephens have known?"

"Y-e-s-s-s, he could have."

"Keep an eye on him," Anika warned. "He could be one of Van Eck's spies."

"Yes, I will have to." Reaching into his waistcoat pocket, Hans' eyes grew large. "My jewels, where are they?"

"Where did you have them last?"

"At the meeting! Van Eck, he must have stolen them in the scuffle!"

"Can you prove this?"

"I'll have to, but how will I have an audience with him to accuse him in public?"

"Offer to meet him at the next meeting and make it plain you'll be selling a tulip of rare pedigree."

"But I told him I would never sell him Anna Fierus."

"And no one said you had to, my dear," said Anika as a wicked smile crossed her face.

"Oh yes, I see now," said Hans, as he too began to smile. "I see now."

"This is truly extraordinary." Nancy was closely examining the coin. "The etchings and the way the light seems to glow within the letters—truly extraordinary."

"The colours and the weightlessness of this gem are out of this world." Sam was holding the trident and couldn't take his eyes off of it as he gently turned the piece against the firelight.

"What do you suppose the writings say?"

"Haven't we seen them somewhere before, Nancy?"

"I think we have, but I can't remember where."

"Well, no matter," said Sam. "We've completed one task, but we still have to see where the tulip mania gets Hans, and we have to see what happens to Anna and Jonathan, so I think we need to find a place from where to watch the De Bruin house."

"Yes, and someplace where we can't be seen by Jake!"

"We need a disguise," Sam said, "and I know just how to do it!"

It was nightfall as the cousins slipped outside and headed down the now quiet street to Hans' house. Light and laughter spilled out from the taverns that occupied many corners, and the gas lamps that had been lit cast an orange glow over the street in small pools of light. The cousins pulled the cloaks they wore tightly around them. The hats they'd taken from the tavern were large and broad-brimmed. Using charcoal from the fireplace, they had pencilled thin moustaches and beards on their faces and had shoved pillows under their cloaks to give them a rather portly appearance. From a distance, the slim, athletic cousins were unrecognizable.

"This time, Sam, if Jake trips you at least you have lots of padding!" Nancy joked as they moved carefully along the street.

"Very funny," Sam replied sarcastically.

They had a clear view of Hans' house from the shadows of a neighbouring house, so they stopped to watch. They didn't have long to wait before a young man appeared opposite and started throwing pebbles against the window on the second floor. Almost immediately a young woman opened the window.

"Jonathan," she whispered, "what are you doing?"

"Anna, I had to see you. Our fathers got into a huge fight tonight. It was all over a tulip that might not even exist! I had to make sure you were all right."

"I'm fine, Jonathan, but I overheard Father saying he thinks your father stole some valuable jewellery from him during the fight."

"Stole some jewellery? How absurd! Why would the richest man in all of Amsterdam stoop to steal some jewellery?"

"My father is convinced of it!"

"Maybe this is my chance to win favour with him and win your hand by returning the jewels if my father stole them."

"I'm sure if you could do that my father would see you in a much more favourable light."

"And I could ask him for your hand in marriage!"

"Sh-h-h-h, someone is coming. You have to go now."

As Anna shut the window, Jonathan slipped into the shadows so as not to be seen. The door to the house opened and Jake appeared on the front steps looking up and down the street. Seeing nothing, he went back inside. As Jonathan walked away, the cousins continued to look up at the De Bruin home.

"Look at the top of the house!" Nancy exclaimed breathlessly. "Can you see it?"

"It's the etchings!" Sam said.

Sure enough, all along the perimeter of the shield, which was held by the two plaster soldiers, and surrounding the lion were the etchings.

"Now I know where we've seen them!" Nancy said. "And I remember they also were on the stained-glass tulip window in the turret."

"We need to keep an eye on this situation," Sam said as the cousins walked away.

"Yes, it seems our little theft has touched a raw nerve, and the magic may be deeper in the De Bruin family than we imagined," Nancy said thoughtfully.

"And maybe our family too! We can't give the jewels back, because we must take them home. But how can we not ruin the De Bruin fortune if they need the jewels to prosper? Oh boy, what a tangled mess." "Let's get some sleep. We have to spend some time tomorrow trying to remember where else we might have seen the writing from the jewels."

Sam and Nancy headed toward the tavern, following canals that had been ingeniously created by diverting the River Amstel using a series of dams to create a network of waterways.

"I wonder who first thought up the idea of using waterways to take the place of carts and horses?" Sam mused as they walked along.

"Much of Holland is actually reclaimed land from the sea," Nancy answered. "These canals were originally built for defence of the city. You can see all around us that new canals are being dug. These canals won't be finished until 1660, but when they are done, they'll cement Holland's reputation as the world's leading trading nation. That's why the period of time we're in is known as the Golden Age of Holland."

"We know all about shipping along the canals, don't we." Sam grinned, remembering their narrow escape.

"We sure do," agreed Nancy, returning his grin. "I bet that Patron Van Eck would have loved to have gotten his hands on those uniforms! He probably has a hand in building these canals, too."

"Yes, this canal project is truly massive, and the canals seem to go on forever in large rings from the centre of the city outwards," Sam said. "Easy to get lost, especially at night."

The cousins continued to walk along the canals, the black water looking cold and uninviting.

The buildings they were passing were narrow in width and deep on the lot; most had back gardens or courtyards where the owners grew vegetables and tulips.

"These houses seem very grand," said Sam.

"They're all very practical, though." replied Nancy. "Although they're adorned with beautiful architectural features, these houses serve a very practical purpose as warehouses and small factories. You see, Sam, the Dutch of the seventeenth century were primarily merchants and traders. They would buy goods and then store them in their homes to either sell at a higher price or make something out of. If you look up to the roof, you'll see a crane used to raise goods from the ground to the upper floors. Much of the lower floor was devoted to business, but the upper two floors were living space. Families like the De Bruins had luxurious living quarters, and with property on the canal, they had preferred access to the shipping lanes."

"He also has a fantastic garden in the back, perfect for cultivating his tulips," Sam said as he glanced over his shoulder.

"Yes, he does. It could be one of the many reasons Van Eck wants to get his hands on Hans' property so badly." Nancy also glanced over her shoulder.

"Someone is following us, aren't they, Nancy?"

"I think they have been ever since we stopped in front of De Bruin's house."

"We need to give them the slip."

"I have an idea, and it's something we're good at, Sam. See all these boats tied up on the canal?

It's time to get wet! When we turn the corner, slip over the canal wall and into the canal. Hang on to the other side of the boat and pray that whoever is following us doesn't hang around."

"This is going to be freezing, Nancy, but let's do it. Just be careful you don't wake the sleeping crew!"

As soon as the cousins turned the corner, they sprang into action. Dropping over the side wall, they entered the icy canal water in silence and hung on to the gunnels of the boat, with their heads just barely above the water. And not a moment too soon, for seconds later a pair of robbers who had been following the cousins came around the corner, the knives in their belts glinting silver in the dark night.

"Where are they?"

"They couldn't have gone far, not with that fat belly on the one!"

"Blast, that looked like our meal ticket. A quick slit of the throat, and the body tossed into the canal."

"Search the boats; we have to find them."

Heavy footsteps were heard on the deck as the thief jumped onto the boat.

"Who goes there?" demanded the ship's captain.

"The owner of this," replied the robber, pulling his knife from his belt.

"Well, get by *this*," answered the sailor as he pulled a sword from his belt.

As the fight began, sailors and boat owners poured onto the boats, which were tied up in a line. It was a huge uproar, with bodies flying all over and men just fighting with anyone who happened along. It was complete chaos! And in the massive brawl, no one noticed two people climb out of the water and run down the street toward the tavern.

"Looks like we did it again!" said Sam as the cousins sat beside a fire warming themselves.

"We just seem to be attracting danger," agreed Nancy. "We just avoided being mugged."

"Yes, seems we just can't go wandering around after dark," Sam said, grinning.

"I thought you were supposed to be protecting me," Nancy teased.

"Other way round, cousin," Sam replied. He winked at his companion, who was already starting to fall asleep, "Other way round." He turned the oil lamp down and soon was in a deep sleep.

CHAPTER 11

PATRON VAN ECK WAS reading the note that had just been delivered when his son Jonathan came into the room. "Look at this, Jonathan," Van Eck said triumphantly. Jonathan took the note and began to read:

Monday, January 25, 1637

Patron Van Eck,

It has come to my attention that Anna Fierus is to be auctioned at the merchant guild this Thursday. As I am quite certain Hans De Bruin will not sell it to you, I would be pleased to be your agent at the auction and trick De Bruin into thinking someone other than yourself was the buyer. Of course, I would appreciate a small fee as a token of your appreciation.

Yours sincerely, Stephens.

"What does this mean, Father?"

"It means I can obtain Anna Fierus and sell shares in the bulb and make a fortune! And I can teach that upstart De Bruin a lesson in business he will never forget!" Van Eck answered with a wicked smile. "Take this reply immediately."

Monday, January 25, 1637

Meet me at the Golden Dragon back corner tonight at 7:00 p.m. to make our plans, and don't dare to double cross me or you will pay for this with your life.

"Right away, Father." Jonathan left for Anna's house happy that he could see her but torn with a sense of disloyalty. How could he withhold information from Anna, knowing his father intended to take advantage of her father? On the other hand, how could he betray his own father? As he approached the De Bruin home, a sense of anxiety and dread began to overcome him. He mounted the generous steps and rang the bell.

"Yes, what is it?" Stephens stood at the door.

"My name is Jonathan Van Eck. I have a message from my father for Stephens."

"Give it to me."

"May I see Herr De Bruin?"

"Step inside; he may have time to see you."

Stepping inside the home, Jonathan had to allow time for his eyes to adjust to the lower light. Typical of many canal homes of the seventeenth century, the lower floor was dedicated to commerce; after all, many of the Dutch were merchant traders. The De Bruin home was a large tailor business. In the centre of the room were rows of benches at which twelve tailors were at work sewing garments. Along the walls were bolts of fabric and other supplies. To the rear of the building, large double doors opened up onto a courtyard where finished goods were being loaded onto carts for transport to the waiting vessels that would travel the canals until they reached the deep water port at the harbour. A narrow flight of steps led to the family residence on the floors above. It was there Jonathan knew Anna lived. He was thinking of her when Jake returned.

"The master will see you. Follow me."

"Thank you." Jonathan felt his pulse quicken. What should he do? He felt like running away.

The residence above was simply stunning! After the industrial look of the warehouse, the family quarters were ornate and finished to a high degree of craftsmanship. The plaster walls were painted a light yellow, and the trim work was generous in size and painted a cream colour. The floors were covered with heavy carpet. Stephens led the way to a door and knocked twice.

"Enter!" The voice sounded stern.

Jonathan went through the door and found himself in the family sitting room. The pale blue walls were covered in artwork, and the large fireplace covered the end wall. A glass door was opened onto a balcony that looked out onto a garden. The furnishings were covered in rich fabric, and the wood tables were dark and ornate. On the mantel, a gold clock began chiming eleven, and the figurines on the side lifted small hammers to ring the bell. Amid this splendour, the master of the house sat in a large chair with his wife, Anika, beside him. Four eyes seemed to bore a hole through the young Van Eck.

"And what would a Van Eck want from me?" Hans asked the question in a pleasant if not overly friendly manner.

"I had come to deliver a note from my father," Jonathan replied.

"Where is it then?"

"I have delivered it to Stephens, your butler."

"Stephens? A note from the patron to Stephens?" Hans looked at Anika, a hard look of understanding crossing his face.

"And why have you delivered this note but then come to see me?"

"Sir, it is with great respect that I ask if I may court your daughter, Anna."

The room was quiet except for the ticking of the clock. Anika sat back in her chair, her mind quickly calculating the Van Eck fortune that Anna could marry into. Hans stood to his feet.

"Court my lovely Anna? How dare you ask such a thing! All the while my jewels are not yet cold in your father's pockets, and he sends you as a spy?"

"No, sir! I'm here because I love her! I know nothing of any jewels, nor am I here at my father's request. I was to deliver the note to Stephens and leave. If my father knew of my intention to court Anna, he would surely lock me up and never let me leave."

"I don't believe you. A Van Eck never can be trusted."

"What can you leave us with that would convince us to trust you?" Anika had finished her calculations and was thinking of an angle that would benefit her.

"Tonight, Stephens will be at the Golden Dragon to meet with my father. They have a plan to take advantage of you at the tulip auction and are meeting to work out the details."

"Are they indeed?" Hans pretended this was a surprise.

"If what you say is true, we may consider your request." Anika was concluding the conversation. "Good day to you, and don't let Stephens know what we have been discussing. He will let you out."

As Jonathan was preparing to leave, the door opened, and Anna came in. Her eyes grew a size larger as she saw Jonathan in the room with her parents.

"Jonathan!" she gasped.

"He was just leaving," her father said.

"Sir. Madam. Anna." Giving a slight bow from the waist, he left.

"And how long have you kept this secret from us?" Anika was stern.

"For a little over a year, Mother."

"A Van Eck! Of all people. We will discuss this further, but your portrait sitting is scheduled, and the painter is in the study waiting for you."

"Is it that fellow Rembrandt?"

"Yes, of course it is. All the wealthy families have him do the painting. Now go!" Anika left no room for discussion and turned her back to look out the window. Her mind was calculating!

"Oh, he is such a fussbudget! I can't stand these portrait sittings. When can we talk about Jonathan?" Anna was asking her father as they walked down the hall to the study.

As they opened the door, her father simply said, "Later. Herr Rembrandt, my daughter, Anna, is here for her sitting."

The painter stood in the centre of the room impatiently tapping his brush against the easel. He was not a large man but was overweight with wild hair and intense coal eyes.

"Come sit by the window. I want the light to fall perfectly on your face."

There was a chair by the window, and Anna did as she was asked. After she was seated, Rembrandt had her move slightly until he was satisfied.

"How long is this to take?" Anna asked.

Rembrandt studied Anna for a few minutes before speaking to her. "I see sadness in your face. Maybe a misplaced love?"

"Not misplaced, sir. I'd rather die than live without him, but I fear my father will never approve of my betrothal, because our families have been in conflict for decades."

"A familiar story, I'm afraid. Just last month I finished a portrait of a young man, the son of a wealthy merchant, who had the same expression on his face as you have."

"Who was he?"

"The son of Patron Van Eck. Jonathan was his name."

"Jonathan! He's the one to whom I'm secretly betrothed. He came to see my father today but was sent away!"

"I see," the painter said. "He was determined to win your hand; he told me as much."

At this, hope began to rise in Anna's heart. Maybe she could have her heart's desire after all.

"Hold that thought now, Anna. The expression on your face is exactly what I want." Rembrandt began painting quickly. "I finish my portraits at my own studio. I have the Van Eck painting there, as the patron tried to lower our agreed upon price, so I have refused to give him the painting of his son. He has threatened to ruin me; he is such an evil man. Mark my words, no good will come to him, and you should be careful around him."

"But Jonathan is so much different; if only father could see that."

"When I'm done my paintings, bring him to the studio, where both will be on display side by side. Perhaps then he may soften and allow the wedding." *And*, thought Rembrandt, *pay for the other painting and allow them to hang side by side.*

Such a talented man, Anna thought. *Maybe he'll be famous one day!*

CHAPTER 12

*I*N A DARK CORNER of the tavern, Jake and Van Eck were scheming.

"So you're sure you weren't followed?" Van Eck had demanded of Jake as soon as they were seated.

"Yes, sir, no one is aware of our meeting."

"And you're sure Anna Fierus is up for sale?"

"Here's what I know. De Bruin is going to place a different tulip into the auction to trick you! It will be called Anika Fierus and will be listed as A Fierus, but I have a plan to trick De Bruin."

"What is it?" Van Eck leaned forward as he said this, his eyes glinting at the thought of a double cross.

"Hans doesn't know I'm working for you, so he'll entrust the tulip to me. I'll switch the real Anna Fierus before the auction so that Hans will *think* he has sold

Anika Fierus, but he would have sold you Anna Fierus for a fraction of its worth!"

"Brilliant!" Van Eck stroked his beard as he said this, and his lips parted in a thin smile that made his face look like a snake.

Sitting in a booth unseen by Van Eck and Jake, Sam and Nancy heard the entire conversation.

"What shall we do?" whispered Nancy. "Hans is walking into a trap."

"We'll be working that night at the auction," Sam replied. "We can switch them back again."

"If we're caught, Van Eck will have us thrown in jail!" Nancy grabbed Sam's arm. "It's so risky with Jake around."

"We'll have to create a diversion for just a moment and then do the switch." Sam had a determined look on his face as he said this. "We must do this for Hans and our future families."

Jake and Van Eck finished their drinks, and as Jake walked by, Sam and Nancy shrank back into the booth. Neither Jake nor Van Eck was aware that their conversation had been overheard. The auction was that night, and Van Eck was already thinking of how he would rise proudly and announce the sale of shares for his rare purchase.

"Are we prepared for the sale?" Hans asked his friend Van Hoff at the auction.

"Yes, my friend, Anna Fierus has been switched for Anika Fierus, and the bait is set to trap Van Eck."

As the auction of tulips began, there was an excitement in the room and the bidding was fierce. Soon, shares began trading back and forth at a furious pace. Sam and Nancy watched the process with fascination. The first tulip sold for twenty guilders to a member of the guild. As only a small number of merchants could buy, the other people who wanted to own the bulb had to wait in the gallery, which was named the stock exchange. Soon an agent, called a broker, appeared before them.

"I have the right to sell the bulb known as 'Grand Duchess,' granted to me by the owner, a member of the merchant guild. What am I bid for the shares?"

"I bid you twenty-two guilders," called out a merchant in the crowd who was known as 'Black Cat' to his friends.

"Sold to you!"

Black Cat was pleased and immediately told the broker to resell them. The crowd was anxious to cash in on the amazing profits to be had with the buying and selling of shares, this brand-new financial invention, so the bidding carried on.

"Twenty-three!" a man called out and bought the shares, giving Black Cat an immediate profit.

And on it went until a final price of twenty-five guilders was reached, and that seemed to set the high price for that bulb on that night.

"No matter," the broker told the final bidder, "the shares will find a buyer at a higher price next week, because after all, what can be more valuable than a tulip?" All agreed this was so in this strange and exciting period of time when the sky seemed to be the limit for the price of a single flower. Many years later, this period would be known as The Golden Age of Holland.

And so it went through the night, with the merchants on the floor buying the actual bulb and then reselling that same bulb for a profit the same night. But there was mischief afoot behind the auctioneer. Jake had blended into the shadows in his usual manner. He had told Hans he would guard his bulb. What Hans didn't know was that Jake had switched the bulb back at the house and had replaced it with the real Anna Fierus, the rare bulb that was gaining a reputation. The auction was progressing well, and word had spread to the merchants that the share sales were hot, and prices were rising. Action was heating up, and Van Eck was anticipating his windfall. The time came for Hans' tulip to come up for sale, and the auctioneer motioned for the bulb to be produced. Jake was carrying the bulb out to the auctioneer when he tripped and went sprawling onto the stage. The bulb went flying out of his hand and skidded across the floor. A young woman server quickly gathered the plant and put it back in the pot. The merchants all rose to their feet and quite a commotion ensued.

"Is the bulb unharmed?" one shouted.

"Who is that clumsy goof?" another called.

On it went as the auctioneer and other knowledgeable merchants inspected the plant to satisfy themselves that its value was unaffected. But this seemed to cause anxiety among the buyers and there was reluctance to bid the price up.

Van Eck smirked as he caught Jake's eye. *Perfect*, he thought, *just as we planned. Drive the price down and then the bulb will be mine for less.*

Jake appeared contrite before an upset Hans De Bruin, but inside he was pleased with his deception. *I pulled it off and now the profit will be mine to share*, he thought.

"Did you make the switch?" Sam asked.

"Yes, I did," Nancy answered. "Van Eck will buy the wrong bulb."

The sale of the bulb went through for one hundred guilders, and the merchants thought Van Eck had done well—that is, until the share auction began.

"What am I bid for Anika Fierus?" asked the broker.

"Anika Fierus is not worth more than fifty guilders," said Black Cat. "And I will bid only thirty."

At this, the bidding stalled, and the bulb was sold for thirty guilders to Black Cat, who speculated that the pedigree could be worth something when he tried to resell the shares later on. Such is the nature of speculation.

"How is my bulb sale going?" Van Eck smugly asked Jake.

"I have bad news. The sale of the bulb was thirty guilders."

"Thirty guilders! That's a loss!" Van Eck was shaking.

"Yes, sir, it appears the bulb was not Anna Fierus, but Anika Fierus." Based on the look on Van Eck's face, Jake wondered if Van Eck would kill him on the spot. "I simply can't understand how the switch didn't work."

Van Eck looked over at Hans, who was being congratulated by a crowd of merchants.

"Well done, Hans! Your first tulip sale and the high price of the day!"

"And who would have thought Van Eck would be the one to pay such a high price?"

"Thank you all," said a modest and proud Hans.

"Soon you'll all be able to view and bid for the finest tulip Holland has ever seen, the beautiful Anna Fierus." Van Hoff said this looking straight at Van Eck. "No man has produced such a tulip! The crimson and orange flames seem to leap from the petals. Kings will want this tulip for display in the royal gardens. It is a prize above all others!"

This created such a buzz in the room that all the events of the evening fell to the wayside. Seventeenth-century Holland had many events to mark it as a most unusual period. The period of the Golden Age birthed a new wealthy class of people, known as the merchant class. Trade was high and the possibility that every man could obtain wealth marked the first time in history this had happened. In order to show their wealth, many built beautiful homes that were richly decorated and furnished. Clothing was elaborate for women, and men dressed in new attire that showed them to be prosperous business merchants. But the strangest occurrence of all was the buying and selling of tulips. This trend, which started between kings of Persia, had been growing and growing, because it showed that excessive wealth could be lavished on luxury, and the creation of a stock market allowed people to buy and sell a tulip without ever having to actually take the bulb home! This created even more excitement when a truly rare bulb came up for sale. What the Dutch didn't know at the time was that the flames on the petals were actually caused by a virus that had infected the bulb, so the tulip would never again grow the same, but this wouldn't be known for many years.

"Seems like a good time to get back to De Bruin's house to replace Anna Fierus," said Sam.

"I have a better plan," said Nancy. "We can help Jonathan win over Anna's father! Listen closely."

CHAPTER 13

"YOU SEEM TO BE in a good mood." Anika was looking at her husband.

"Yes, our plan to deceive Patron Van Eck worked! He bought Anika Fierus for three times what he was able to sell the shares for! And we made a profit of one hundred guilders and the admiration of all the merchants at the auction!"

"It is good." Anika gloated as she began to think of the gold jewellery she could buy. Her thoughts were interrupted by a knock on the door.

"Sir." Jake was at the door. "Jonathan Van Eck is here to see you. Shall I send him away?"

"No, Stephens, I'll see him."

"He will see you in the study," said Jake warily. "Why are you here? Did the patron send you?"

"It is of no concern to you," he said dismissively. "I know the way to the study."

As Jonathan stepped into the study, Hans stood up to greet him.

"So you were right—your father did set out to lower the price of Anna Fierus. But we tricked him!"

"Sir, I'm afraid that there is treachery in your household!" And with that, Jonathan threw open the study door. Jake, who'd been leaning against the door to listen, fell into the room.

"Here is the man who switched Anika Fierus for Anna Fierus. He is working for my father!" Opening his cloak, Jonathan produced Anna Fierus, which had been given to him earlier that evening by Sam and Nancy with instructions to return it to Hans.

Hans towered over the cowering Jake as he looked down at him. "Is this true, you viper?" The words were filled with questioning rage.

"No, they are all lies," Jake replied, pointing a boney finger at Jonathan. "It is he who stole Anna Fierus this very evening and is trying to win favour from you."

"Then how do you explain this?" Jonathan said as he grabbed Jake and reached into his pocket. Holding the ring and the trident in his hand, he gave them to Hans. Jake hadn't noticed that when Jonathan had picked him up he had placed the jewels in his pocket. Sam and Nancy's plan was working!

"My father paid you with these jewels for the switch."

At this, Hans couldn't control his rage. Looking at Jake, his hand gripped the fire poker he'd been holding, and with a swift blow he brought the metal rod down on Jake's head. Jake fell heavily to the ground, the blood from his wound pooling on the floor. He lay perfectly still.

"Is he dead?" a shocked Jonathan asked.

"What have I done?" moaned Hans as he slumped into the armchair. "I'm a murderer."

"Quickly now, pull yourself together. We must act," said Anika. "If word of this gets out, you'll go to prison and we'll be ruined. Take this carpet and roll him up in it; we'll dump the body into the Amstel River and it will float out to sea."

Together the three conspirators rolled the body of Jake up in the carpet.

"Quickly now," Anika said, "take him downstairs and through the warehouse to the canal and be careful none of the other servants see you."

Moving quickly, Hans and Jonathan carried Jake through the house.

"There's a wheelbarrow in the garden just outside of the warehouse," Hans said, pausing to catch his breath.

"Go and get it and we'll wheel him through the warehouse to the canal."

They were sure they hadn't been seen, but from the shadows of the warehouse two pairs of eyes watched.

"Do you think we were caught?" An embarrassed lady's maid asked. "If they knew we were together down here, we'd be fired!"

"I don't think we were," the sly footman replied. "It seemed they were up to no good, but what were *they* doing?"

"Yes, what were they up to?"

"I'll follow them to see. This might be our way to climb out of our station in life and move upward."

"Yes, I agree. We've been servants for generations and know all kinds of scandals the rich have been involved in, but never have we been in a position to use it against them! The class system has held us back, with little chance to save enough to start a business of our own, but maybe now we might have something to use to our advantage and not be servants for life."

"I'll follow them." Giving the maid a quick kiss, the footman began to shadow Hans and Jonathan.

The night air was crisp, and the streets of Amsterdam were deserted when Hans and Jonathan carried their load to a waiting boat in the canal. Silently rowing through the canals, they reached the first of three dams that held back the Amstel River. Looking around to ensure no one was watching, they took a drill from a toolbox in the boat and bored a hole through the bottom of the hull. The vessel slowly began to sink. Climbing ashore, the two men pushed the boat into the current and headed for home.

"You must never say anything of this to anyone. You know I didn't intend to harm the boy, but who would believe me?" Hans was deeply shaken.

"There's only one way to assure yourself of that," replied Jonathan. "Give me the hand of Anna in marriage."

"And your father? What will he do to my lovely Anna when he learns of the marriage? He will be furious and can be vindictive."

"I have a plan, if you'll trust me." Jonathan looked directly at Hans as he said this.

"We're in a deep conspiracy now. What other choice do I have? Tell me your plan."

CHAPTER 14

As Jonathan and Hans crept back to the house, Sam and Nancy emerged from the shadows.

"Quickly," Sam said, "I must get Jake from the boat in case there's a chance to save him."

Already the current was slowly dragging the boat lower and further out to sea. Sam, being a strong swimmer, quickly shed his shoes and coat and dove into the icy water. Nancy followed along the canal edge, prepared to help when she could. Little by little, Sam pulled the boat closer to shore. He was exhausted but wouldn't give up because he knew if there was even a chance Jake was alive, he had to make it to where Nancy was anxiously waiting. Finally, he was able to toss the rope to Nancy, who helped pull the boat to one of the ramps beside the water. Sam dragged himself out, and with the last bit of strength he had, helped Nancy pull the blood-stained carpet with Jake inside onto the bank of the canal.

"Sam, you are so strong; all that surfing has paid off. I'm afraid to look inside the carpet, but I have to."

"Thanks, Nancy. I'm grateful there were loading ramps along the shore to use."

Slowly the cousins unrolled Jake and, much to their relief, discovered he was alive.

"I don't like him," said Sam, "but we saved him from drowning."

"I agree," Nancy replied, "but now we have another problem. What do we do to keep him away from Van Eck? He will surely tell him that Jonathan is working with Hans!"

"What a mess!" agreed Sam. "How did he ever find us here? He must have special powers for evil."

"One thing is for sure, we have to get him out of the way."

"I have an idea," said Sam. "What if we hide him in a crate in the warehouse at Van Hoff's business? I remember there were hundreds of them. By the time he's found, we should be in the clear."

"Let's move then; it will be light soon, and we have work to do."

The cousins threw the carpet into the river and untied the sinking boat. Soon both were drifting downstream and slowly submerged beneath the black water. This time, Sam and Nancy had no trouble with guards on the dock, as they were sound asleep. Finding a crate, they put Jake inside and fastened the lid down.

"I am so tired," Nancy said. "The sun will be up soon, and we agreed to meet Jonathan at the Golden Dragon."

"He has a lot of explaining to do." Sam was aching all over after his evening. "And I need some dry clothes and a few hours of sleep."

"Father?" Jonathan approached Van Eck who was at his desk.

"What is it?" Van Eck growled.

"I have news that the bidding for Anna Fierus is going higher than ever before."

"And why is that?" Van Eck glared at his son.

"It's rumoured that the king himself desires it for his collection."

"And where did you hear this?" Van Eck asked sharply.

"I was listening in on a conversation between Van Hoff and a merchant tulip trader known as Black Cat," Jonathan lied.

Van Eck paused for a moment. This was important news. If the king wanted the bulb, it would sell for a fortune! He must have it!

"Have you seen that fool of a butler Stephens?" Van Eck asked.

"No. Why would you need him?"

"He owes me good information. Find him if you can."

"And if I can't?"

"No matter, I'll bid the highest before the auction has even begun." Van Eck stormed from the room, determined to own Anna Fierus.

CHAPTER 15

It was February 15, 1637, and the winter air was cold as Hans De Bruin walked from his lawyer's office. He had never been happier.

"Hans!" Van Hoff had stopped Hans in the street in front of the Golden Dragon where Sam and Nancy were seated and waiting for Jonathan. "Is it true what I heard of Anna Fierus?"

"What have you heard?"

"That it has been sold before the auction?"

"Yes, it's true I sold it today and am just now returning from the lawyer's office where we completed the bill of sale."

"But is the price to be believed? I heard it sold for an entire city block of buildings!"

"Yes, my friend, that is the price."

"But that's incredible, Hans! That makes you Amsterdam's wealthiest man! This must surely mark the height of tulip trading. Who was it that paid such a price?"

"It was Patron Van Eck."

"Van Eck? He was the one? What was he thinking?" Van Hoff was incredulous as he said this.

"I have no idea what he was thinking, but I've made sure I was paid and that he couldn't cheat me. The deed to the land is here in my pocket! Yes, I agree, this surely will be known as the tulip bubble!"

"What good fortune for you. Let us have a drink to celebrate!"

"Yes, of course we will, my friend; after all, I owe all my good fortune to you, for you rescued me from ruin when Van Eck wouldn't buy my uniforms. I will be forever grateful." Taking the jewels from his pocket, he looked at them. "It seems good fortune has returned. I received a letter today, asking me to join two strangers and Jonathan Van Eck at the Golden Dragon. We will celebrate later."

"You will meet with the son of Van Eck? Can he be trusted?"

"I will see."

Sam and Nancy were waiting for Hans at the Dragon. As soon as he saw them, he remembered them, for Nancy had released him from the power.

"I know you!" he said. "I saw you long ago at my farm, and at the auction, but you haven't aged at all!"

"That is so," said Sam, "for we are time travellers. But we also know of your secret. Stephens is alive!"

"Alive? How is that so? That's such good news, but so dangerous for me." Hans looked worried.

"Don't worry," Nancy said, "your secret is safe with us, but you must go and rescue him from Van Hoff's docks, where he's hidden in a crate. We put him there so that you might conclude your business with Van Eck."

"How can I repay you for your secrecy?"

"There are three things you must do to ensure our silence," Sam said. "First, you must find Rembrandt and pay for the painting of Jonathan and gift it to your daughter at her wedding."

"Her wedding?" Hans said this looking downcast.

"Yes, her wedding," Sam continued. "Second, you must find Jake, who you know as Stephens. We locked him in a crate on the docks, and you must send him away on a ship, never to return to Holland."

"All right, I'm happy to do that part," said Hans.

"And third, you must always keep the secret of the jewels safe in your family and ensure they are passed down through the generations. If you do those three things, we'll keep our silence."

Eager to have his secret kept, Hans agreed to all the cousins' conditions. Then he hurried to Van Hoff's dock to find the crate and release Jake.

Later that night, Van Eck sat alone at the auction. He wasn't alone by choice and was nervous. Word of his purchase had spread, and all the stock traders were on edge. Concerned that the value of a tulip had finally reached such outrageous heights, they realized that surely there had to be an end to the madness. They all knew that stock prices only go up when there are more buyers than sellers, and as they talked among themselves, they realized that not one of them would be willing to invest an amount greater than the fortune Van Eck had spent. That night not one person showed up to bid. The bubble that would be known in time as the Tulip Mania had finally burst. Van Eck looked at his purchase, Anna Fierus. The intoxicating beauty of the bulb stood in stark contrast to the deepening gloom in Van Eck's mind. *I'm ruined*, he thought. *I must go to my bank and take the money out before word of this gets out and people begin to panic and withdraw all of their money.*

Van Eck hurried to his bank, but as he rounded the corner, he saw that a crowd had gathered in front of the bank. It was a run on his bank as depositors, aware of his blunder and fearful they may not be able to withdraw their money, clambered for their savings. Worried bank employees had barricaded the doors, afraid the mob would tear them limb from limb.

"There he is!" cried a member of the mob. "There's Van Eck."

"Give us our money!" And the crowd gave chase.

Afraid for his life, Van Eck began to run toward the docks, the screaming mob in hot pursuit. Aware he would be torn to pieces, he ran into the docks and hid among the crates.

"Who's there?" The voice inside the crate sounded familiar.

"Stephens? Where are you?"

"Over here. Get me out!"

Van Eck opened the crate, and a beaten and bedraggled Jake emerged.

"You!" Van Eck cried. "You are responsible for my ruin! I should kill you with my bare hands."

"You fool!" snarled Jake. "Stick around and the crowd will do that to both of us. And don't call me Stephens; my name is Jake."

As he spoke, the angry mob arrived on the dock and started searching.

"You better get Van Hoff," said an alarmed dock worker. "This is getting ugly."

Van Hoff arrived on the dock with Hans, who had come to release Jake but was unable to get to him before the crowd arrived.

"Friends, stay calm. What is your business here?"

"We're here to find Van Eck! His bank has closed and barricaded its doors, and we fear we'll lose all of our money."

"What makes you think he's here?"

"We saw him come this way."

Hans stepped in. "Friends, do not destroy the merchandise on this dock belonging to Van Hoff. You know he's a good and fair man who doesn't deserve to lose everything because of a scoundrel like Van Eck. As you may have heard, I have acquired most of Van Eck's assets. I will own his bank soon as well and will guarantee your money. It will be safe with me. Now go home, and we'll find Van Eck."

The leader of the mob spoke up: "Yes, what De Bruin says is true. Let's go home now. Van Eck will soon be found."

"That was a close one," Nancy said to Hans as the crowd began to disperse.

"I have some bad news, though," said Sam as he joined them. "Jake has escaped."

"I can't imagine either will show their face in Amsterdam again," said Van Hoff. "Hans, you have some further business?"

"Yes, I have a wedding to announce and a debt to a painter to pay." Turning to Sam and Nancy, he looked directly at them. "Will you come and work for me? I have a large empire to run, and your skills would be valuable."

"No, I don't think so," said Nancy. "We kind of have an appointment to keep closer to home, but there is someone coming into your family who will be a great addition."

"Yes, I guess you mean Jonathan Van Eck. I think he will join our family business as head of trading."

"I couldn't think of a better fit! I'm sure you'll treat him as a son. I heard that you were very generous with your wife's maid and your footman. Is it true they were given enough money to marry and move to France?"

"Yes, they were very loyal to us. It was Anika's idea that they move away."

"Must have been terrific employees." Sam smirked as he said it, remembering the couple in Hans' warehouse.

"Do you think we'll meet up again?" Sam asked as they walked away.

"You never can tell!" Nancy said with a smile. "One more thing to wrap up—let's go and meet up with Jonathan at the Golden Dragon and give him the good news. I think his marriage to Anna is going to be magnificent."

From under the tarps on the small boat that was heading toward a large ship in the harbour, Van Eck and Jake were watching Sam and Nancy walk away.

"Where are we headed?" Jake asked.

"To England. I need to start again, and you're going to help me."

"But I need to return to where I came from!" Jake said with alarm rising in his voice.

"You are going with me. I can use someone as devious as you to rebuild my empire and return to recover my wealth from De Bruin."

"But you have no money! How will we start again?"

"You are a fool, aren't you? Look at the clothes we're wearing."

Jake took a closer look at the clothes. The buckles were gold! Buttons were diamonds! The cloth had silver threads! The boot heels were solid emeralds! Everything they were wearing could be cashed in! Still, Jake was trapped in the seventeenth century with a villain.

"You do have a plan for England, don't you?"

"Make no mistake, I'll be back to claim what is mine. I hear the current trading ships are going to a colony called America in the new world, so I thought I could cash in."

Jake smiled. "When do we sail?"

EPILOGUE

BACK AT THE TURRET, the professor and the cousins were still talking about the adventure.

"So Van Eck and Jake fled to England." Sam was concluding his memories of the adventure. "But how did he arrive in Amsterdam in the first place?"

"I'm sure he must have caught hold of your coattails, and while you were still groggy from the time travel, slipped into the shadows," the professor answered.

"I'm glad we left him in the seventeenth century," Nancy said.

The professor said nothing but looked into the fire as if contemplating the future.

"You know, the only thing we didn't find was the secret to Anika's gold," Sam said.

All at once, the mantle clock chimed. Nancy walked over to it to examine the delicate bell.

"Look at this," she said, turning to Sam and the professor, "The chime where the hammer hits has turned gold."

The three of them took a closer look at the clock.

"Could it be?" The professor took a small pocket knife out and gently scraped the clock. As the gold emerged from beneath the paint, he began to scrape faster. Moving over to the lion, a simple scrape revealed more gold shining through. "It is true!" he said with excitement in his voice.

"Look what I found in the tapestries," Nancy called to the other two. "Real gold and silver threads."

All at once the cousins and the professor began scraping small bits of paint off all the contents of the turret, and before too long the room was dazzling with gold and silver. The lion on the mantle had rubies for eyes and silver for claws. The unicorn on the mantle was solid gold with a silver horn and emeralds for eyes. Even the inlay metal on the chairs was gold.

"Anika's gold!" exclaimed Nancy

"And it was here all along!" said the professor.

"And one last thing to look at," said Sam, who was investigating one of the large rocks on the fireplace. In the gold and silver glow of the room, an inscription began to show up.

"This inscription," Nancy said, "is the same as the writing on the stained-glass window."

Nancy pushed the rock with the inscription on it and the wall opened on a hinge, revealing a large chamber. Nancy was the first to walk inside, Sam followed, and the professor, who could not believe his eyes, was last.

"Anika's treasure." He could scarcely breathe.

The cousins just stood there amid the largest collection of seventeenth-century precious artifacts ever seen, but best of all was a single gold nugget set into a ring, with the inscription, "For Anna."

The air was electric with anticipation at the unveiling of two undiscovered works of art. After the professor had valued Anika's treasure, he decided to gift the portraits of Anna and Jonathan to the Rijksmuseum in Amsterdam. After months of debate, experts had decreed them authentic Rembrandt paintings.

"I think it's only fitting that Anna and Jonathan continue to be together," Nancy had said.

"Yes, it's wonderful, as it would have been a shame to have them sold separately and split apart after how difficult it was to help them get together."

"Yes, our ancestors have quite a history, but much of it can never be told!"

"With the power of the jewels, the family had to run the business to new heights, and Jonathan did a good job of building up the trading empire. He and Anna had four children of their own and even let Anika come to live with them after Hans died."

"I don't understand, though, how the De Bruin family name was passed down through Anna."

"Anna did marry Jonathan Van Eck, and because Hans had been so good to him, and his own father was exiled in disgrace, Jonathan chose to honour the De Bruin name by having his children carry it."

"How did you come to obtain the paintings, professor?" asked Sam.

"Not to mention Anika's gold!" added Nancy

"The paintings and the business were passed to the eldest son of Anna and Jonathan, who was given the name Samuel. No one in the family could understand why that name was chosen, but Jonathan insisted on it. This began a long line of descendants, many of whom were given the name Samuel, who built the De Bruin empire over hundreds of years until it had grown to include shipping, automobile manufacturing, diamond merchandising, and, of course, garment manufacturing. The secret of the jewels remained within the family, which stayed in Holland until Samuel's son, Alfred, sensing peril from the growing war in 1939, began to convert the family's wealth to gold and send it to an aunt in England. She held it until Alfred joined her in April 1940, just one month before the German army invaded Holland. He brought with him only one suitcase with his clothes and two very precious jewels. He remained in England throughout the war but supported the Dutch resistance financially. When the war ended, he moved to the USA with his English bride, Kate, and some wonderful antiques. He proceeded to build a new business in diamond merchandising, which he passed along to his sons."

"So it was Alfred De Bruin, my grandfather, who brought Anika's paintings to the USA," Sam said as he pushed a lock of blond hair out of his eyes.

"No, it wasn't your grandfather who brought the paintings," said the professor with a twinkle in his eye, "but he brought the jewels that hang around your neck. The paintings were brought back by my grandfather, who built the school!"

"And also, Anika's gold!"

"Indeed. There was more than one surprise in Granddad!" The professor chuckled as he said this, obviously delighted.

"Sir," an attendant said, "the unveiling is about to begin. May I introduce you to the museum curator?"

A young man in his early twenties stepped forward. He had black hair that was a mass of curls and a slightly elongated face that was unpleasant to look at. He was examining the portrait. He stuck out his hand as he turned to face them.

"My name is Jacob Van Eck. I believe you know my ancestor, Jonathan." A diabolical grin spread across his face.

The End (or is it?)

ABOUT THE AUTHOR

*J*OHN GOWANS IS A retired investment advisor who lives in Victoria, British Columbia, Canada. Together with his wife of forty-seven years, they have three married children and seven grandchildren.

"I hope you've enjoyed reading my first book, and possibly learned a bit about a truly unique period of time."

The tulip mania of seventeenth-century Holland was a real event. At the height of the mania, a single bulb was traded for a city block of real estate. Many of the references to building styles, canal uses, and dress styles are historically accurate; however, the characters are completely fictional. As for the magic coin … you never can tell! I hope you join me for the next journey when Sam and Nancy go on their next adventure!

Manufactured by Amazon.ca
Bolton, ON

18168820R00081